MW00412277

Mystery Along the

Danube

The Forgotten Jewel

A Rosetta Blessing Mystery
Book 1

All rights reserved
Copyright © 2018
Published 2018
Second Edition 2019
With additional photos
Graphics by A. Nation Books
ISBN: 9781799148357

A. Nation

Copyright

This is a semi-fictional book. The boat tours, the weather conditions, and sights along the Danube are real. The main story, the book Rosetta is reading, and her mishaps are fiction.

A. Nation

Table of Contents

Mystery Along the Danube

More Books by A. Nation:

Visit A. Nation's Amazon page:
http://www.amazon.com/A-Nation/e/B00SUHXM6E
to see what books are currently on sale.

Cast of Characters:

Harry Brown
Rosetta Blessing
Joyce Blessing
Hans Becker
Mr. Heyburn
Alfredo
Mario
Marco
Tom
Viceroy Henry Edmond
David Smithy

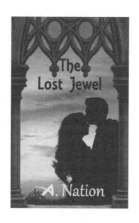

Acknowledgments

I want to thank those that gave me support and tolerated my persistence in writing my story; they are by first names only as they know who they are: Write on the Edge group,

Helen, Shirley, Christie, Kam, Nancy F., and John

Preface

Greed does funny things to people. Some take out of love to impress, others take to satisfy their worth. This is the first story of the Rosetta Blessing Mystery stories incorporating my travel experiences into her mystery books. Like many of us, we tire of our daily jobs and need a change. Rosetta has the chance of a lifetime to visit faraway lands and in the process, do the right thing.

In an age long ago, the wealth of a man either was judged by how many lands he conquered or betrothing the women from his tribe to wealthy kingdoms. Sometimes, gifts of great value are exchanged as representing a symbol of sovereignty. When they are lost or stolen, the owner may have no proof of power over his land or the tenants.

As centuries and generations pass, wars obliterate titles and ownership. What if there could be a way to restore the grandeur of ages gone by?

Chapter 1 - Harry Brown

Harry Brown, dressed in his khaki suit, shivered as he stepped out of his car to look up and down the vacant street. He pulled the front of his fedora hat down in case someone drove by and recognized him. Nighttime and overhead clouds already cloaked the city in darkness except for the dim corner street lights.

Sirens in the distance. He turned his head to the disruptive sound, then relaxed when he realized they weren't coming his way. Smoking the last bit of his cigarette, he withdrew the white cylinder from his lips and threw it into the gutter. He ran across the empty two-lane street and entered the pay phone booth. Making this call would change the rest of his life. He didn't want to use his cell phone while he called his buyer.

The wiry chain smoker planned the biggest deal in his sorry rotten life. His hit and miss income forced his girlfriend to give him an ultimatum. She told him she found employment in Maryland and he better get a steady paying job or she'd leave him. Since they first met, he tried to tell her his income wasn't steady, but that didn't sit well with her.

"Yes, I have it," Harry Brown said into the payphone receiver. "Pay me first, and then I'll send it to you. You owe me. Good. Hang on. I need to check my account."

In his life, Harry dealt on and off with loan sharks and a few scams of his own until he came across this medieval tale searching one day on the internet. After several contacts with book dealers, he hit the jackpot. A remote bookseller in upper state New York had what Harry hoped to find. He drove from Chicago to Latham, New York and called on the store owner. Purchasing the diary for a good price, lower than the seller wanted, he soon found a buyer in Europe.

If this exchange went down according to his plan, he could settle into a respectable life in the Bahamas with his girl. Under the dim light of a distant street lamp, he fumbled to open his cell phone with his other hand. Only wearing a light jacket, he shivered in the cool night air as he connected with his bank account. He held the payphone receiver next to his ear and remarked to his contact.

"There's only half here. You said you'd transfer all of it," he barked. "Fine, but I better get my money by next week. I'll send it. Don't you worry. Look, there's an all-night postal service a block from here. You should get it in twenty-four hours. Hello? Damn." His party had hung up.

Harry slammed the pay phone receiver down into its carriage. "I'll show him," he mumbled. He opened the diary and tore out several written pages from the back end. Harry stuffed them into his left pants pocket as he stepped away from the phone shelter. A drizzle of raindrops dripped on his face as a breeze sent a chill through his thin frame. He clutched the small book in his jacket pocket, as he glanced back and forth down the empty street before dashing down the wet sidewalk.

He wrapped his wet hands around the cold damp doorknob and entered the all-night Express Postal store. As he opened the door, a loud ring jangled above from a bell in the silence of the night. A startled older woman jerked up from a crouching position behind the counter.

"Yes, may I help you?" she asked, reaching for the alarm button hidden under the register.

"I-I need to mail a package overseas," Harry stuttered from the chill in his wet clothes.

"Let me see it," she said, hovering her finger over the alarm button.

Harry pulled out the small book from his wet nylon jacket. The clerk motioned him over with her free hand.

"That has to be wrapped or boxed," she said.

"Do you have a box this would fit in?" he asked.

"Yes, it'll cost you."

"Just wrap it good. I can pay," he said as he dripped rainwater on her faded carpet from the brim of his hat.

Frowning, she pulled out a foldup box from underneath her counter and adjusted the book to the outside panel to make sure the book would fit.

"Address?" she asked, turning the flat of the cardboard box toward him.

He picked up a pen with a plastic flower stuck to the end from a jar filled with glass beads and wrote down his benefactor's address in large print. Tearing off a sheet of notepaper from the counter, he wrote a note he wanted to insert inside the box. *"You'll get the last five pages when I'm paid in full,"* he wrote. Folding up the small brown and white box, he placed the diary inside with the note and closed the self-sealing lid.

"Lay it on the scale," she instructed.

The clerk withdrew her hand from the side of the counter to write down the weight and priced it from the address he wrote on the side of the box.

"What's the highest amount I can insure this for?" he asked.

She looked at him in the eye.

"Anything hazardous or fragile?" she asked.

"No, it's—" he began and looked at her. "You just saw it was a book," he growled.

"I'm required to ask," she replied, glancing again at the address on the wrapping.

She glanced again at the address on the wrapping."Hungary? Do you need insurance?"

"Yes, yes I do. How high can I get?"

"Hmm, as a book, it shouldn't be much."

"Whatever. Can you hurry? I have an appointment."

She raised her painted eyebrows and tilted her head.

Harry could tell she didn't believe him but at this point, he didn't care.

He watched her move through the motions of setting his package on the polished silver scale again. She opened her logbook to determine the cost for overseas shipment.

"Air and ground shipping is about twelve fifty. That insures up to one hundred dollars."

"What's the highest I can insure it for?" he asked, shifting his feet from one foot to the other as he tried to stay warm. He turned sideways to glance through the window for anyone passing by.

"Sir?" she said, calling for his attention. "You can pay seventy dollars for a thousand dollar coverage."

"No more?"

"That's it. Credit card only," she replied, standing firm.

"Fine," he snapped and after a few moments of searching his back pockets, he handed her his credit card. He had paid over two thousand dollars for this diary.

"Place your card in the machine by your wrist and sign your name in the display window."

He did as instructed. She waited until the card processed. Stamping the package with the postal marker, she placed an insurance sticker next to the forwarding address. A paper ticket spit out from her machine. She tore it off and handed the thin paper to him.

"Here is your receipt. You can track it with this number," she said and circled the code on the slip with her pen.

He watched her as she placed his package behind her on top of a larger box in a canvas bin.

"Anything else?" she asked, staring at him.

"No, I mean yes," he replied, folding his receipt into his pants pocket next to his keys.

He shoved his hand into his other pocket and withdrew the torn pages from the small book. Harry picked out an envelope from the nearby rack that matched the size of the loose pages. He inserted them inside before peeling the protective paper off the glue area of the envelope. He pressed down and sealed the flap. Borrowing the flowered pen again from the cup on the counter, he printed his address on the back left top and center.

"I'll need this mailed," he said, handing the envelope to the clerk.

She gave him the price for the envelope and the stamp.

"Insurance?"

"Seventeen fifty," she replied.

"I'll pay it," he said.

He pulled out his wallet, but this time he handed her a twenty dollar bill. Once he received his change, he rushed to the door. Opening it just enough to stick his head outside, he looked up and down the sidewalk for those he knew worked for the local loan shark. Not seeing anyone, he stepped out onto the wet pavement of the sidewalk. As the door swung closed behind him, the abrupt ringing of the bell overhead made him jump. The rain had let up a little, but the mist in the air kept the streets damp as he ran back to his parked car, splashing a puddle into the air.

As he pulled his key from his pants pocket, his receipt slipped out and fell on the trickle of water flowing over the pavement. Just as he tried to retrieve the moistened paper, a gust of wind picked it up and set it onto a larger stream of water heading for the gutter. Harry ran after the slip of white paper until he watched in horror as his proof of mailing sailed on the gutter stream and disappeared down through the bars of the street drainage.

"Nooo," he cried under his breath and stomped his foot in a puddle.

His action threw the water up, covering his pants leg. Clenching his fists, he thought, *"I'll get a copy in the morning."* He didn't want to wait here any longer. He had enemies and he didn't want them to catch him out here exposed. He glanced up and down the street to make sure no one had witnessed his mistake, he ran back to his car. After a few swear words while sitting in front of his steering wheel, he pulled out his cell phone and confirmed his tickets he had left on hold from his favorite travel agency in D.C. Once he gave the male voice on the other end his credit card information, he threw his cell phone into the center console. Turning on the ignition, he started his vehicle before he sped down the street.

By the time he drove to his apartment complex, the spattering of rain had stopped. He parked his car on the street. He rushed up the apartment's steps before glancing around for anyone approaching him. Pressing a code on the grimy keypad over the doorknob, he entered the dim foyer.

Before the front door closed behind him, a man entered. Harry ran up the stairs. As he tried to unlock his door, steady footsteps from more than one person climbed the staircase behind him. A hand grabbed his shoulder and jerked him around.

"Who are you?" Harry asked, shading his eyes from the hall lights glow behind the man's head.

"Shall we go inside, Mr. Brown?" said the tall man, holding Harry's arm.

Harry didn't recognize the man's graveled voice. Another large man stood behind his assailant in his hallway. The one who spoke to him turned his door handle and pushed him inside his apartment.

"What do you want? I don't keep much money here." Harry whined.

He frowned, trying to think of an escape. *"How can I escape? Were these men from the local loan shark? It's too soon to pay the money he used to buy the diary."*

"We want the book," the taller man growled.

"Book? I don't have it. It's not with me," he pleaded.

"Who else knows about the diary? Who are these guys?" he asked himself as his thoughts raced for a solution.

The second man stepped forward, shoving him down into the well-worn sofa.

"Where is it?" he growled into Harry's face.

"You'll never find it," Harry barked back.

The first man's head almost touched the ceiling. The crannies in his face betrayed his rough years. Harry watched him go into his bedroom while the shorter of the two stood over him.

"If I could throw something at them, I might make it to the open doorway," Harry thought.

He shoved his hand into the seam for something between the cushions. But he wasn't fast enough. The roar of the man's gun filled the apartment. The pain in his stomach at first didn't register.

The man searching in the bedroom ran back. "What'd you do that for?"

"I thought he was reaching for a gun," the other bruiser said, holding his weapon.

Feeling cold as he bled out, Harry watched the first man bend down and pull on Harry's weak arm. A TV remote tumbled to the floor from his weakened grip.

The older man slapped his partner across the face.

"You fool, he just had a remote. Come on, let's get out of here," was the last thing Harry's dying brain heard.

Chapter 2 - Rosetta

Travel agencies are one of the important functions in Washington, D.C. Like a smooth running Lexus, the agencies run the comings and goings of congressional representatives and foreign delegates to their destinations. Three airports in the district accommodate every traveler and tourist needs.

Rosetta Blessing, supervising over twenty-five employees at the Washington Travel Agency franchise, struggles to catch up on her work while answering questions from the new crew. The young employees needed a week of training to learn the finer points of servicing their VIP customers. *"Why had her boss hired extra employees in this economic strain?"* she wondered. She guessed the hiring may be a result of high turnovers most employers experience with the younger generation. *"No sense of loyalty,"* she thought while sliding several approved reservations into their envelopes for the daily pickups.

Most of the agency's work entailed, booking reservations at hotels, flights over the phone, and preparing travel package plans from online orders.

Rosetta, now in her middle fifties, worried about her age, her grown children, and running the agency in an efficient manner.

Looking up from her backlog of paperwork, she saw one of the newest employees, Mary walked right into the manager's office without knocking. Mr. Heyburn not only was her boss but the manager of the Washington franchise.

"I'll have to talk to her again about protocol in this office," Rosetta thought, pursing her lips together as she sifted through her documents.

Five minutes later Mary sauntered out, attracting many male employees before sitting down at her desk. Rosetta rose up, straightened her waist vest with her fists, and marched over to the errant employee.

"Mary, may I have a word with you?" she asked, standing in front of the employee's desk.

The woman's blue eyes stared up at her supervisor. A strand of blond hair curled over her forehead.

"What is it Mrs. Blessing?" she asked, brushing her blond hair from her eyes.

"Mary, would you please come over to my desk," Rosetta said before she turned to walk back to her station.

Mary put her pen down, stood up, and straightened her snug yellow dress. Her high heels gave off loud clicks to the tiled flooring as she walked by her co-workers. All eyes from the nearby male employees watched her swaying hips as she followed Rosetta across the room.

"Have a seat," Rosetta said, gesturing toward the chair beside her desk as she sat down.

"What is it you want to see me about?" the woman asked, smacking her jaw as she chewed on a stick of gum.

Rosetta winced upon hearing the motion and sound of gum chewing.

"Mary, please don't chew gum in the office."

"Sorry, Mrs. B," she replied, removing the substance from her mouth with her long red fingernails and depositing it into Rosetta's trashcan.

Rosetta stared and sat firm, crossing her fingers together on top of her desk.

"Mary, it is the protocol of this office that if you need to talk to Mr. Heyburn, you must come to me first. You can't just go marching into his office without an appointment, and please address me as Mrs. Blessing," Rosetta explained.

"Wow. All right, I'm sorry. I haven't worked in a fancy place like this in a long time," Mary said, crossing her long nyloned legs.

"Well, now you know. You may return to work."

The young woman rose from the chair, straightening her tight dress. Rosetta added one more piece of advice.

"And, Mary, please wear something more conservative for a working office," Rosetta added.

"Yes, Mrs. Blessing." Shrugging her shoulders, she headed back to her desk, swaying her hips all the way.

The office work continued booking airlines for VIPs, reserving their hotel rooms, and ship destinations. This routine continued in the office until Rosetta asked her new employees for the Vanders' file.

"Please, people look in your file trays. Mary, have you seen the Vanders' file?"

When Mary returned that 'doe in the headlights look,' Rosetta couldn't contain her frustration.

"I don't understand you people. Can we have a resemblance of order around here?" she shouted.

Her boss, Mr. Heyburn, poked his head out of his doorway. Embarrassed by her own reaction, Rosetta apologized in front of everyone.

"I'm sorry, Mrs. Blessing. I'll find it for you," Mary said and looked through her incoming tray. Not seeing it there, she located the file in the outgoing tray.

All was quiet until another employee mislaid a senator's plane tickets to London. Incidents, one after another, arose until Rosetta lost it again. This time she ran to the bathroom to keep the others from noticing her eyes swell up with tears. She didn't want Mr. Heyburn to think she couldn't handle training the new crew. She didn't want to lose her job over a few mistakes by the new employees.

Recovering, she returned to instruct everyone to stop what they were doing and look for the tickets. The search took most of the afternoon until another employee located them in one of the desk drawers. She breathed a sigh of relief. A few minutes later, Mr. Vanders' secretary walked in to collect the tickets.

At five o'clock sharp, Rosetta was more than ready to go home. She gathered up her coat and purse before she rushed out of the office as fast as she could.

Rosetta fought the congested parkway traffic until she drove down the off-ramp to a neighborhood grocery store. Purchasing a few items, she took the local avenue home. Relieved when she turned into her driveway, she parked her car and pressed the garage door remote. Sitting for a moment, she rested her head in her left hand. She wiped a strand of her graying auburn hair from her face as she waited for the garage door to open. She was exhausted. The fatigue wasn't the type of weakness a person gets from physical work but an emotional toll which had built up over time.

Rosetta hated to admit to herself she didn't have the desire to carry this heavy work burden any longer, but at the same time, she wasn't ready for retirement yet. Her repetitive instructions and watchdogging the employees at work wore on her. The enthusiasm she once had from this job she loved now seemed like a distant memory.

"Good thing today is Friday and only one more short day of Hell," she thought with a heavy sigh. As soon as her

garage door rolled up, she drove her car in. Once parked in the single car garage, she turned off the ignition, pulled out the keys, and gathered up her purse from the passenger seat. Maneuvering her large frame out of the car, she stood and jerked her waistcoat into a straighter position. She opened the trunk of her car, gathered up the few groceries she purchased earlier,and headed for the kitchen door.

She pressed her key fob to lock her car and flip the switch to close the garage door. Since learning about another stolen car in her neighborhood from the local newscast, she made sure everything was secure. Rosetta located her house key and entered her seventies-styled kitchen of painted cabinets and linoleum flooring. A twenty-year-old refrigerator stood near the long Formica counter around the sink. Magnets and works of art from her grandchildren decorated the fridge. Rosetta could afford a new refridgerator or a kitchen remodel, but she was comfortable with the vintage setting. She would rather spend her money on something fun.

She lived alone. Her daughter and son, now grown, lived elsewhere in town. This quiet time allowed Rosetta to have this afternoon as one of the few moments she enjoyed for relaxation.

Her daughter, Joyce, who graduated from high school, attended the local college and moved out to join her friends a few miles away as their roommate. Joyce's passion involved her love for rock climbing and history. Rosetta admired her lack of fear and ability in the sports mall, but she still considered it a dangerous sport.

Her son, Bob, her oldest, married with two children of his own, lived twenty miles on the other side of town. Though her children are not far from her, she sometimes wished they were small again, running around the house. Those were happy and yet trying times.

Rosetta divorced her husband, Stan, many years ago when the children were small. He was one of those men who believe he's always right and everyone around him is wrong. When he began placing security cameras, double locking the doors, and spying on the neighbors every time they were outside, she put her foot down. The last straw came in the grocery store when he couldn't find her. He yelled and ranted in front of fifty or more people before she could quiet him down. All he had to do was call her on his cell phone.

After two more episodes of this behavior, she finally said 'no more' and told him to leave or she would. He left easier than she thought he should. Working for the local power company he spent his money on his hobbies of electronic gadgets, leaving little left over for Rosetta and the children. A year later, Rosetta filed for divorce and received alimony for the children.

At the time of her separation, Rosetta worked in a health insurance company, processing state insurance forms. When a friend of hers retired from the travel agency in D.C., she applied for the supervisory position. The larger salary she earned helped her look at her bank account with a smile and put her children through college.

Rosetta hauled in her groceries to the kitchen and placed the perishables into the refrigerator. The rest, the soup cans and cracker boxes, she stacked on the pantry shelves in the cupboards. While she restocked the shelves, she heard the back doggy door flap. In ran her small brown terrier, Dolly, who jumped up and down to greet her.

"Oh, all right, you deserve something for being by yourself all day," she said, petting Dolly's head.

Dolly circled her human twice.

When Rosetta reached into a bag of dog kibble and offered her a couple of treats, her dog stopped prancing and wolfed the snacks down as fast as she could.

Rosetta rushed into the master bathroom. She couldn't wait to take a long soak in a warm tub. She poured a few drops of lavender bath oil into the rising water. Dolly followed her into the bedroom and jumped on the bed. As the fragrant aroma filled the bathroom, Rosetta reached behind her head to undo her long light brown hair from the bun she wears while at work.

Undressed, she walked to the tub, turned the faucet off, and eased her aching body into the warm fragrant waters. After a long period of soaking, she rose out of the tub water with great reluctance. Drying herself off, she pulled on her favorite tshirt and wrapped into her cloth bathrobe. Rosetta towel rubbed her long hair before sitting down to brush it out at her vanity.

Dolly jumped off the bed and trotted after Rosetta. Ignoring her dog, Rosetta returned to the kitchen to make herself a cup of hot chocolate. She carried it into the living room, and set the steaming cup on the small table near her favorite blue chair.. She exhaled a long sigh as her back and leg muscles relaxed throughout her body, raising her spirits.

She settled back into the recliner and reached for her book resting on the side table. Dolly jumped up into her lap. She recalled the story began with an old count after he lost his wife, Rosetta drew out her paper bookmark. She adjusted Dolly in her lap and began reading the fictional historic tale about the lifestyles in early Europe.

"Katheryn?"

"Goodnight, father," she called. "I'll see you in the morning."

Discouraged he walked down the stairs. The count entered his study and poured a cup of wine. The old warrior of sword battles long gone stepped close to the dying embers of the grand fireplace. Easing himself into his favorite chair, he ruminated about his heritage. His hair, long and gray, framed his haggard features. He didn't know what to do after his wife died a few years ago. Now, left with only one heir, he decided he had to force Katheryn's hand. What good were his victories in battle and his title, if he hadn't a way to bequeath his earthly goods? His only choice was through his daughter and her future marriage.

In the coming days, Count Gawain decided to contact his old friend Henry Edmond who held the title, Viceroy. The count remembered Henry danced at least one dance with Katheryn on her birthday. The count appealed to his friend. If he offered his daughter's hand in marriage, they can, in return, use their combined lands to strengthen both of their powers over the populace. *"He would be perfect for Katheryn,"* he mused.

When he fought to protect his people from the Cossacks years ago, the local tribes offered him their loyalty and the surrounding land. He, in turn, presented the township a beautiful necklace from his spoils as a show of his allegiance to various groups of villages along the great river. The jewels represented his status and power. He allowed the farmers to remain and work his lands. In return, they would hold out a percentage of the crop as their payment to him. Without this feudalistic arrangement, he would lose control of his territory.

Standing, he approached his bureau and withdrew the jeweled necklace. The old man's finger stroked the golden metal's reflection along the necklace until his finger slid around a reddish orb. He received this jewel from a local chieftain for saving his life. This was his inheritance to pass on to his daughter's family. This bejeweled necklace secured his lands and his subjects.

20

He had to find a way to marry off his daughter. His age convinced him, he didn't have much time left.

He had hoped by now his daughter would have wed and bore him several heirs. *"She has been so stubborn and willful of late,"* he thought. *"I blame that heretical printing machine from Germany. I'm glad she reads the Bible, but the other books her friends bring into this house give her ideas. By God's Thunder, I wish her mother was still alive today."*

With great care, he folded the soft red cloth over the jeweled adornment and laid it in a dark mahogany box. Locking the small container, he set it into an open drawer of his private bureau. Inserting the vintage key into his vest, he pulled a laced shelf skirt over to hide the facing of the drawer. At that moment, his daughter, Katheryn, barged into his study.

"Father, what is the meaning of this?" she demanded, waving a white scroll in her hand.

"What is it, my dear?" he sighed. Her sudden outbursts had come so often. If only he could run away from her constant complaining. He loved her beyond words, as a father would, but the sooner he married her off, the better for all concerned.

"This, this letter from Viceroy Edmond. Were you planning to speak to me about this?" she asked, holding out the rolled stationary with the wax stamping peeled away.

"Let me see," he said, grabbing the envelope from her hand. "You shouldn't read my letters, dear Katheryn. Hmm, I see my old friend is coming to visit."

"Yes, and you told him, I would make a perfect wife. You can't make me. I won't marry that old derelict."

"You have to marry some time or the Elector of our local religious order will send you to serve our Lord in the convent. And then where will I be without heirs? Where would you be without the security of your inheritance?" he lamented.

"All you think about is yourself. I want to marry for love, father. I have no love for Henry Edmond. Besides, he'll probably die in our wedding bed of heart failure."

"Better that way than before. By the date of this letter, he should be here any day. I want you to be on your best behavior when he arrives," the count said, folding the letter. Reaching up, he set the scroll of paper on top of his chest of drawers.

"Father," Katheryn said, softening her voice, "I have a confession to tell you."

"Eh? What is it?" he said, turning to look at her

"I love someone else. I can have many children with him," she confessed.

"Love? Love is just an infatuation. Marriages bind land, families, and seal agreements. One doesn't marry for love. Who is this person? Someone with greater lands than the viceroy?" he asked, throwing his hands into the air.

"Yes, people do marry for love. I have heard of such stories from the musician in the village," she said, lifting her chin in defiance.

"Fiction. That's all they are. And I'd advise you to put away your childish thoughts. Henry is coming for a stay and you shall marry him," he proclaimed.

The count watched as his daughter's mouth pressed into a frown as she gathered her broad skirt and ran out of the room crying. He must stand firm, he told himself or his peers would judge him with disfavor. If he couldn't control his daughter, how could he maintain his tenant's loyalty and lands from any future invaders from the north? *"No, she must marry the viceroy,"* he decided.

Rosetta Blessing licked her finger and turned the page.

The day had arrived. The viceroy's carriage, pulled by four white horses, rolled to the front steps of the castle. A servant, dressed in a black waistcoat over puffy white knee trousers, stepped out of the manor's heavy wooden front doors. Noting the well-dressed footman standing near the back of the carriage, the doorman offered his assistance.

"Here, announce this to Count Gawain," the Viceroy said, handing over his hand-printed calling card.

Once the doorman read the printed name, the young man handed the card back to the elder guest and sprinted back inside to alert the count.

"Count Gawain, the viceroy is here!" the doorman yelled as he walked through the hallway. His voice reverberated against the stone walls over and over again.

"I'm coming. I'm coming. You can quit shouting, my lad," the count replied, entering the grand foyer to greet his domestic. "Well, don't just stand there. Go help the viceroy bring in his cases, hurry."

Count Gawain walked toward the open wooden doorway and watched as his and Edmond's servants hauled in baggage, a carved wooden chair, and single feathered mattress. Travelers brought all their belongings for long stays. Guest rooms in most castles were barren of furniture and bedding. Some guests even brought their own wood to light the room's fireplace.

"Henry, my old friend, so glad to see you once more," said the count, rushing to embrace the viceroy. They had fought together in the battle when the Cossacks invaded from the north of Europe.

"I am glad to see you, too," the Viceroy replied, returning the hug to his friend. "Where can my servant place my things?"

"Boy," the count called to his doorman, "Lead the way for the viceroy's servants. You, my friend, please join me in my study for some wine, or would you prefer ale?"

"Ale, my friend. Thank you for inviting me. This manor is magnificent," the Viceroy said, admiring the stucco figurines attached to the walls.

"Yes, yes, now follow me," the count said, leading the way into a smaller room to their right. The viceroy followed his friend into a furnished room warmed by the lighted fireplace. "Now, where is your daughter?" he asked, patting his old friend on the back.

Rosetta turned the page and placed a torn scrap of paper into the book's gutter. Without realizing it, she had been twirling her hair between her fingers. A strand fell across her eyes. She paused and wiped the loose hair over her ear. She stretched out her arm and grasped the handle of her hot cocoa cup from the narrow table stand beside her chair.

The hot beverage, still warm, relaxed her before she opened her book again. As she was about to continue reading, the doorbell rang, followed by a series of knocks. Her daughter, when she was young, loved to announce herself after school with her secret tap code. Rosetta would pretend on the other side of the door to ask for a password. *"Oh, those were the fun days,"* she thought. When she heard footsteps entering the hallway not far from her small living room, she bookmarked and closed her book.

"Mom," a familiar woman's voice called out. "Are you home?"

"In here, dear," Rosetta replied, laying her book on her lap. Dolly jumped off Rosetta's lap and barked.

A shorthaired blond woman peeked around the living room archway. She was much slimmer compared to her

25

mother, but all Rosetta saw was the little girl she had raised to be a beautiful young lady. Her daughter squatted down to pet the excited dog.

"I just stopped by to get a few of my things and drop off my climbing gear. Space is tight in my apartment. Oh, here's your mail," Joyce said, entering the room before she handed over the small collection of envelopes.

"You won't need your rock stuff?" Rosetta asked, accepting the envelopes.

"Not for a while, Mom. Are you all right? You look tired."

"It has been a rough day for me. Training the younger generation, exception noted, has been difficult, to say the least. Every workday feels like I'm spending an enormous amount of time on one catastrophe after another. Thank you, looks like a bill here, and more junk mail."

"I think you need a vacation. Your job pays well, and Bob and I aren't living at home anymore."

"Well, yes, I have accrued enough funds in my bank account, but my job. What about my responsibilities?"

"Screw them. Your health is all that matters to me," Joyce said, sitting in the chair near her mother. When she noticed the book in her mother's lap, she had to ask, "What are you reading?"

"Oh, just a book of historical fiction. It relaxes me," Rosetta said.

"What's it about?"

"Life in the fifteenth century. It's actually based on some true events that the author fictionalized. I find these tales are easier to read than boring history texts. Oh, I don't need these," she said to the handful of junk mail she still held in her hand.

As Rosetta attempted to discard one of the brochures in the junk mail into her small waste can. Her daughter grabbed the booklet out of her hand.

"Look at this. You could go on a river trip to Europe and see those stories come to life," Joyce said, holding out the thin catalog.

"Oh, I don't know," Rosetta replied.

"Tell you what, you look it over and I'll stop by Sunday to see what you have decided.

"But I don't want to travel alone," Rosetta whined.

"Well, I could come with you. I'll have to write a thesis next year about Medieval Europe. I would love to see the reality of history," Joyce said, rising from her chair.

"I'll give it some thought," Rosetta replied, placing the brochure on the table near her hot cocoa.

"We'll talk about that on Sunday. In the meantime, I have to pick up some groceries. Is there anything you need?" her daughter asked.

"No, I just made a stop there on my way home. Thanks anyway."

Joyce bent down and gave her mother a kiss on the cheek, and said, "Remember Sunday."

"I will, about one o'clock?" Rosetta asked.

"Yes, I'll see you then," replied Joyce.

Rosetta heard her daughter run upstairs to her former bedroom and after a few minutes, she walked downstairs, hurrying out the front door.

She picked up the riverboat brochure with the picturesque scene of the three-deck boat on the water against the background of the European mountains. Checking the back of the booklet where her address was stamped, she set the brochure, this time, on the coffee table. She picked up her cup and drank the last of her lukewarm cocoa before she continued reading her book.

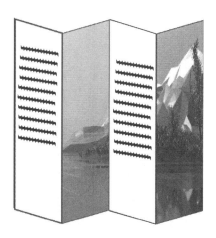

A. Nation

Chapter 3 - Tickets

Saturday morning, unlike her other workdays, extended until three o'clock. While she drank her coffee, Rosetta glanced over the riverboat brochure before setting it on the kitchen table. Gathering up her purse, she headed through the door into her garage.

Upon arriving at work, she was relieved that most of the part-timers were not in attendance. Mary and a few of the men sat at their desks answering the phones and filling their reservations. Just as she decided to ask her boss for time off, Mary walked over to her desk.

"Mrs. Blessing, I have unclaimed tickets. What shall I do with them?" she asked.

"Oh, honestly, Mary, just put them in the Late Pickup box. Someone is bound to claim them." she sighed. On one hand, Rosetta was glad the new employees asked questions, but Mary seemed to have a memory problem with easy tasks.

The day progressed without disasters. Five minutes to three o'clock, she decided this was the right time to talk to Mr. Heyburn about taking a vacation before he left. She rose out of her chair and knocked on the open office door near the imprint of his name in the upper center of the door, 'Mr. Heyburn, Manager.'

"Come in, Rosetta," he said.

A. Nation

Rosetta walked in and sat on one of the chairs beside his desk. A pen set and photos of his family adorned the top of the carved oak desk.

"Yes, Rosetta, what can I do for you?" he asked as he reached for his heavy jacket on the coat rack.

"Sir, if you could you spare me a few minutes, I really need to talk to you."

He turned toward her placing his hand on the back edge of his leather chair. "Yes, Rosetta, what is it?" he asked.

"Mr. Heyburn I need to talk to you about me taking a vacation. I have the time accrued, and it looks like things are beginning to run smoothly," she blurted out.

"Oh, you do? Well, I have noticed you have done a remarkable job with the new employees, with that exception from yesterday.

"Well, yes, there's Mary. Everyone else has a handle on their jobs. Do we really need an extra employee in this office? She doesn't seem to be too qualified."

"I know she may be slow to learn but give her time. She's a daughter of one of my friends," he said, clearing his throat. "You know, in businesses like this in Washington, we accept grants. If we don't use the money, we lose it for next year. If she doesn't work out, I'll put her in for a transfer later on."

"I see," Rosetta said, waiting for his reply to her request.

"As for your vacation, it has just come to my attention we have a couple of non-pickups in the Late Box. One of them was an online order from, let's see—" he said, shuffling through the papers on his desk. "Yes, a Mr. Brown. I have been notified that he is no longer with us. He died and didn't leave us an alternate recipient to claim them. See, the story about his demise is front page news in the paper."

31

He shoved the morning edition over his desktop toward her. Rosetta glanced at the headlines and a photo of police cars in front of an old apartment building.

"Sorry to hear, sir, but what does that have to do with me?" Rosetta asked, pushing the newspaper back toward him.

"It's two non-refundable tickets for fourteen days in Europe. Take someone with you."

"But—"

"No buts, take it," he said, handing her the sealed envelope.

She hesitated. "Tell you what. If no one claims them by next week, I'll take them. But I have to think about this," she replied.

"Fine, but this chance only comes through here once in a long while. I'd use it, but my brother's wife is having their third child, and I promised I'd keep her husband entertained. You'll have to decide quickly. The tickets times are scheduled for a flight that leaves this coming Thursday. I'll keep them in my desk drawer in case you change your mind. You could take Mary for the company," he suggested.

"I want to think about this," she replied, dreading the thought of her and the employee spending time together. Joyce would be her first choice.

"Of course." He looked at his wristwatch and back at Rosetta. "I see it's almost three o'clock. Let me know on Monday what you have decided. Have a good evening," he said, rising to retrieve his coat from the clothing pole behind him.

"Thank you, I will think about it and let you know one way or the other," Rosetta said and rose from her chair.

A. Nation

She definitely didn't want Mary hanging around on her vacation. Working all the time, she hadn't developed many close friends. Her thoughts turned to Joyce, who showed an interest from the brochure she received.

Sunday, Rosetta tended to her housekeeping chores and vacuumed the carpets. The tantalizing trip to Europe invaded her mind. Dolly followed her wherever she went except when Rosetta wheeled the vacuum cleaner out into the living room. After the dog's constant barking at the noisy machine, Rosetta picked up the terrier and set her outside into the backyard.

"I'll have none of that," Rosetta said and shut the back door in her dog's perplexed face.

After she watched through the door window to make sure Dolly wasn't going to return through the doggy flap, Rosetta headed back into the hallway to finish her vacuuming. When the clothes washer finished, she pulled her damp clothes out and pushed them into the dryer. Noting the time from the small wall clock, she thought she'd better eat some lunch before Joyce arrived.

Before she could look in her refrigerator, her cell phone rang. The screen displayed Mr. Heyburn's name.

"No, I won't answer right now. He can call one of the new employees," she told herself and set her device on the table.

As Rosetta turned off the vacuum and wrapped up the cord. A slap from the doggy flap bumped her back door. She shoved the machine into the closet, as Dolly trotted into the living room, looking around for the noisy vacuum. Rosetta wiped the dust off her television and tackled the coffee table. She lifted a vase of plastic flowers to clean underneath and picked up her cell phone from the table to call Joyce.

"Hi, honey. Say, have you had lunch yet? Perfect, I know a quiet spot out of town. I'll treat. See you in a while."

She slid the brochure and her cell phone into her purse sitting on the sofa. She walked into the bedroom and sat down at her mirrored vanity. There she brushed her graying auburn hair to one side. Wrapping her long tresses around her head, she secured it into a bun with a clip. Dolly whined.

"I'm just going out for a short time. You'll be fine," Rosetta assured.

As she walked back into the living room, she heard a car pull up in the driveway. Peeking through the window drapes, she saw Joyce exit her vehicle. She made sure Dolly didn't follower her as she stepped through the front door into the frigid air.

"I can drive or do you want to?" Joyce asked, approaching her mother.

"Your car is still warm, so you drive. We are going north. I'll give you directions," Rosetta said.

After twenty minutes of driving on the crowded highway, Rosetta instructed Joyce to take the next turnoff.

"How far are we going, Mom?" Joyce asked, turning down the off-ramp.

"It's just a few miles further into Virginia."

"Have you been here before?" Joyce said as she drove down the bumpy country road.

"It's been years if the restaurant is still there, and I need to get out of town."

"What did you do, Mother?" Joyce asked with a smile.

"My boss texted and he wanted me to sub today and I didn't want him to ruin this day we planned together. I haven't answered him yet.

"How would he know you are out of town?" Joyce asked.

"With today's technologies, he could. I just didn't want to call him back while I'm at home. There it is. Pull over by that red pickup."

Joyce pulled over and parked her car in front of a small café with redwood siding.

"So, when were you here last?" Joyce asked, turning the ignition off.

"Before your father and I had Bob. We were so much in love at the time," Rosetta said, opening her passenger door.

"I'd love to hear that story."

Joyce exited her vehicle and locked it before they walked into the small restaurant.

Once inside, the waitress said to pick any spot they wanted. Rosetta spotted a few patrons dining toward the front of the café. She pointed to one of the tables in the back with four chairs. The tables and chairs along with the flooring and walls were all polished pinewood.

"This is lovely, Mom," Joyce said, admiring the vintage pictures hanging on the walls around the room.

The waitress brought them glasses of ice water and menus. Already in the middle of the table, the silverware, wrapped in paper napkins, were stacked in a pyramid.

"I brought this," Rosetta said, pulling the small brochure out of her purse. "I tabbed a few places that looked interesting. But first I'd better make this phone call."

She pulled her cell phone out of her purse and made the phone call to her boss.

"Hello, Mr. Heyburn. I'm sorry I didn't call you right back, but I'm out of town at the moment. Oh, how odd? That's great you found someone to help you. I wish I could come in, but I don't have my car with me. My daughter has spirited me away for a massage and lunch. Yes, that is an excellent

35

idea. I'm sure Mary or one of the others could use the overtime. Yes, I'll see you on Monday. Goodbye."

Rosetta looked at her screen after she had hung up on her boss and began laughing. "Someone came into the office and spilled coffee over a batch of outgoing tickets. Then the person left. How odd."

"Now that's the mother I remembered," Joyce said, sipping some of her cold glass of water.

"What was odd, the man asked for a reservation when it happened. Before they knew it, he ran out of the office."

"Maybe he was too embarrassed. Have you decided on our trip together?" Joyce asked, picking up the travel booklet.

"That's what I want to ask you about. Mr. Heyburn has two dead tickets waiting for my decision.

"Dead tickets? Sounds gruesome," Joyce said, removing her cardigan sweater.

"It's what we call a ticket when the owner has died and no one claims them. It's for one of these river trips in Europe."

When the waitress came back to take their order, Rosetta requested a raspberry margarita.

"Which one is it?" Joyce asked when the waitress left.

"I don't know. I forgot to look, but I do know it's for fourteen days. Someone in the office took the order online. I'll find out where on Monday. If someone does claim them, I'll buy my own. I have to get away."

"We can look this over and decide on a trip if you don't get the tickets," Joyce said.

Their waitress returned with their order and set the sandwich plates down in front of them on the table. She returned and placed Rosetta's margarita off to one side.

Mother and daughter giggled and ate their shrimp and avocado sandwiches. Rosetta told Joyce a few choice stories about her father when she and Bob were little.

"Remember how you used to ride your father's back like he was a horse?"

"Yes, and he would buck me off too. Those were the good old days before he got funny."

"Yes, I think he ingested too much from the newspapers and the TV news. Those reporters just want to stir things up," Rosetta commented and dabbed her napkin around her lips.

Before they realized it, the time slipped away and they knew they had to head back home.

"Oh, Mom. Look at the time. I sure enjoyed this lunch with you. I feel like we can relate without you turning motherly on me," Joyce said.

"You know, I do too. You're so grown up. Come, let's get home. Dolly probably thought we've been kidnapped."

It was five thirty by the time Joyce drove into her mother's driveway. Dolly met them as soon as they opened the front door. Rosetta closed the door and picked up the excitable dog for a hug. The warm home encouraged Joyce to remove her coat and lay it on the sofa in the front room. Rosetta struggled to put her wiggling dog back on the floor before she tried to leap out of her arms. She removed her coat and hung it in the living room closet.

Heading for the kitchen, Rosetta asked, "Would you like some coffee or tea?"

"Tea would be perfect," Joyce said, still rubbing her hands while she blew into then to warm them up.

After a few minutes, Rosetta placed two hot water cups on the table and handed Joyce a tea bag, Joyce noticed her mother's hands shaking.

"Mom, are you nervous about something?" Joyce asked.

"Yes, I've never had this much preparation for an event like this trip since I gave you birth."

They laughed until Dolly started scratching one if the low cupboard doors for a treat.

On Monday, Rosetta prepared the first breakfast for herself in a long time that didn't just consist of coffee and toast. She scrambled eggs, fried two sausages, and toasted a slice of wheat bread. She wanted the energy to tide her over when she asks her boss about the tickets. Even if someone claimed them, she was ready to write the agency a check.

Pulling out the used jam jar from the refrigerator, she brought everything over to the kitchen table. Dolly watched her every move until Rosetta filled her food bowl. After the meal, she deposited the dirty dishes into the kitchen sink and headed back into her bedroom.

Dressed in her waist jacket and knee-high gray skirt, she grabbed her black purse and headed for the garage door from the kitchen. She noticed her stride seemed uplifting today. Dolly's toenails tapped the tiled floor over to her as she jumped around.

"No, you can't come, but I hope to be home early. Bye bye," she said to the terrier as she closed the kitchen door.

She drove on the expressway and arrived a few minutes before the agency's opening time. Already several employees' voices murmured though out the room either soliciting or accepting reservations from travelers.

Rosetta stopped at the receptionist's desk.

"Hi, Suzie, is Mr. Heyburn in yet?"

"Yes, he just arrived."

"Thanks," Rosetta said, before walking toward her boss's office.

She knocked on his open door. When she heard him say "Enter," she walked in.

"Mr. Heyburn, do you have some time?" she asked.

He stood by the coat rack and adjusted his jacket on one of the hooks.

"Yes, Rosetta, what can I do for you?" he asked, sitting in his swivel chair.

"First, I hope you salvaged the mess you had from yesterday. I'm sorry if I couldn't be more helpful for you."

"Not to worry, most of the material was saved or replaced."

"Good, I have thought about those tickets in your desk. Have they been claimed yet?" she asked.

"I don't believe they have." He unlocked the middle desk drawer and checked inside. "Nope, they are still here."

"I would like to use them if I could. My daughter will be joining me. I guess I should ask where the reservations will take us."

"Here, look for yourself." He paused, handing Rosetta two sealed envelopes.

She accepted them and borrowed his letter opener. Slicing the steel between the flap of the envelope, Rosetta pulled out the tickets. After reading the destination, she jerked her hands down and gasped.

"This is for The Grand European Tour. I–I can't believe it. Are you sure this is all right with you, with the agency?"

"Yes, I could see you have been working hard training the personnel and bringing in more clientele. Consider this your yearly bonus and take your vacation time," Mr. Heyburn said.

"Oh, thank you. Would it be all right if I didn't work today? I don't think I could keep my mind on my job effectively, thinking about this."

"Sure, we have a lot more employees working today compared to Sunday. We'll hold the fort down for you," he assured. "Oh, stop by accounting and have them reissue your tickets under your name."

"I will, thanks again," she said, smiling.

After she left her boss's office she glanced around the various desks filled with employees in their cubicles. Stopping at the accounting office, she handed them the tickets.

"Mr. Heyburn gave these to me. But I need them reissued under my name and my daughter's name, Joyce," Rosetta explained.

"No problem. It will just take a moment," the accountant said, taking the tickets from Rosetta's hand.

In a few minutes, he handed her the new tickets. She hurried over to her desk and opened an online chat with the riverboat company. She proceeded to add a day before and after the ticket dates in Budapest and Amsterdam to allow for any delays. Sliding the envelope into her purse, she walked out the door.

The first thing she did after returning home was to call her daughter.

"Hello?"

"Joyce, I have the tickets and you're not going to believe the trip we are taking. Can you come over right now? If not,

I'll wait until you can," Rosetta asked while Dolly danced around her legs.

"I just got off work. Would lunchtime be all right? I'll bring you that deli sandwich you like."

"Okay, see you then."

She tapped on the red icon, closing her cell phone connection. Picking her dog up, she turned around in a circle.

"Oh, Dolly, I'm going on a wonderful trip. Wait—what am I going to do about you? Oh dear," she said, lowering her voice as she set the dog back down on the floor. "I have to call a few friends."

By noon, she still hadn't found a sitter for the little terrier. She didn't want to leave her at the kennel to pick up kennel cough or bad habits. Nor did she want her neighbor to tend her dog, considering the last fiasco when Dolly ran off. Just then, she heard the familiar knocking when the front door unlocked.

"Mom, where are you?" Joyce called out.

"In here, hon," said Rosetta from the bedroom. Dolly jumped back into Rosetta's arms.

Joyce entered the bedroom, glancing at Rosetta's open suitcase, half filled with clothing. Rosetta placed her dog down on the carpeted floor and stood frowning at Joyce.

"Mother, you don't look happy enough to be going on a trip. What's wrong?" Joyce asked.

"I can't find someone to care for Dolly. I'll have to kennel her."

"Have you called Bob, he has a backyard."

"Oh, but he and his wife are busy with their children—"

41

"Nonsense, you put him through college and they have a housekeeper. I'm sure he would take Dolly. The children loved her the last time they came to visit here."

"But I don't want to create a burden every time I want to travel."

"First, let's eat lunch. I'll call him later," Joyce said.

"Thanks, hon. I'm afraid if I called him, I would cave if he said no."

After they ate around the kitchen table, Joyce gathered up the paper trash from lunch. Rosetta gave Dolly a piece of chicken from her sandwich and waited until Joyce returned.

"I forgot to ask you. When do we leave?" Joyce asked, returning to her seat.

"Thursday morning.

"This Thursday! Oh, that's only three days away. I'd better notify my part-time job I'll be unavailable. I'm sure they won't hold my job for two weeks. And I'll have to pack, and get a haircut, and—"

"Now look who's excited. I'll schedule the haircuts. Mine has been a little shaggy of late. You'll have time to return to your school in September."

"Yes, wow, love you, Mom. I'd better call Bob right now."

Her daughter pulled out her cell phone from her hip pocket. "Watch this," Joyce said and made the call to her brother.

"Hi, Bob, this is Joyce. Mom and I have the chance of a lifetime. She's taking her vacation on Thursday. But right now she needs you. Can you babysit Dolly? I know but think how many times, she has saved your butt. It's only for two weeks and— "

Rosetta couldn't hear the rest of the conversation as Joyce stepped out of the kitchen to talk in the living room. After a few moments, she returned.

"Okay, it's all set. He'll come here and pick Dolly up on Wednesday. Then I'll see you on Thursday morning."

"That's great. Why don't you just come over Wednesday night? I'll make dinner, and you can sleep in your old room," Rosetta suggested.

Joyce stopped to think about the arrangement for a second. She said, "Sounds great, oh, I have so much to do. Yes, let me know when we can get our hair cut."

Rosetta followed her to the front door and watched Joyce bound down the front steps just like she used to do as a child.

Chapter 4 — Rosetta's Book

After watching Joyce get in her car through her front window, Rosetta closed her front door and looked down at her dog.

"Now don't you look at me with those big brown sad eyes of yours. You'll have a vacation too," Rosetta said removing her sweater. She placed the cardigan into the hall closet and headed for the kitchen to make a cup of hot chocolate. Humming to herself, she thought she'd read more from her book and brought her hot drink into her small study. Rosetta pulled out her cell phone and called her hairdresser.

"Yes, I need two hair appointments for this afternoon or tomorrow. Three o'clock tomorrow? No earlier? No, that would be fine. Oh, me and my daughter. Can I have Kathy work on my hair? Okay. Yes, Stacy is good too. Thank you," Rosetta said.

After hanging up, she dialed Joyce's phone but got her daughter's voice mail.

"Hi, hon, our hair appointments are tomorrow afternoon at 3:00 p.m. Come a half hour before if you can," Rosetta said.

Satisfied their plans were set in motion, she walked into her study. Placing her hot cup of cocoa on a coaster on the coffee table, Rosetta sat down into her favorite cushioned chair. She picked up the heavy book from the coffee table. Pulling out the bookmark, she began reading the story while Dolly curled up near her feet.

A. Nation

Katheryn ached from sitting a long time on the edge of the stone bench. The bright sunshine mocked her distress. The young woman's shoulders shuttered as she cried. Her finest clothes in her flowered bag lay at her feet She couldn't believe David had forgotten to meet her. She thought his love was true. As the time passed on, she realized he wasn't coming.

She gathered up her heavy flowered bag into her arms, and marched back to the manor. Just as she wiped the tears from her cheeks, she looked up and saw a gilded covered carriage parked in front of her home's front steps. *"Oh, that must be father's friend,"* she thought.

She pulled away a hedge branch to watch two footmen unload the luggage from the back of the coach. Her curiosity got the better of her as she strolled along the flowered path through the garden toward the rear of the mansion. She stopped for a moment when she saw the viceroy enter the mansion with his assistants. *"He looks as old as father,"* she thought.

Still distraught over her lover not showing at their agreed meeting location, she rounded the grounds to enter through the service entrance. She hoped she could avoid watchful eyes of the servants, but the cook jumped when she entered the large kitchen.

"Oh my, you gave me a start, young lady," the older woman said, holding her hand to her chest.

"Sorry, Madeline. You won't say anything to my father, will you?"

"None of my concern," the cook said and returned to stir the large kettle of goulash soup.

Rushing by the cook, Katheryn entered the narrow hallway where she could hang her cloak. Glancing toward the front foyer, she observed her father and the viceroy enter the study. She scrambled upstairs with her luggage in tow.

The next morning, Count Gawain, his daughter Katheryn, and Viceroy Henry Edmond of Bulgaria sat at the table waiting for the servants to bring in the prepared breakfast. The count, still in his dark brown dressing gown contrasted with his daughter's pale pink silky dress.

"Tea, Henry?" the count asked. "I ordered it special just for this occasion."

Henry was impressed, for only the rich could afford the tea's long journey from Lebanon or Portugal.

Count Gawain's daughter's cold attitude chilled the air around him. She sat straight across from the viceroy in her chair, gazing out of one of the tall sunlit windows to her right

The viceroy nodded toward the count. "Yes, I'd like that. Uh, Miss Katheryn, would you please pass the sugar?"

The young woman glared at him and shoved the bowl of the sweetener toward the old viceroy with the flat of her hand.

"Madam, it's a beautiful day out there. Would you care to join me for a walk after breakfast?" the viceroy asked, stirring the hot beverage.

The count, familiar with her bursts of tactless rebuttals, interceded just as his daughter attempted to open her mouth to speak.

"I think that would be a grand idea. Katheryn, why don't you show the Viceroy our stables," he implored, cocking his head to one side.

Katheryn turned to stare at the viceroy.

"Yes, Sir Henry. We can take a walk," she sighed, lifting her chin upward. "But first I must change."

The old count breathed a sigh of relief. He smiled as the servants brought in trays of fruits and meat.

After breakfast, the viceroy waited in the foyer for Katheryn. He knew once they had their walk, she would understand the new position she would enjoy as his wife.

After a while, the young woman made her entrance down the stairs from her bedroom. He noticed she had changed from the broad silky dress of pale pink of the morning meal to a slimmer riding outfit of deep blue.

"Shall we go?" she said, passing him as she led the way through the front door.

Henry had to step fast to keep up with the young maiden.

"Over here is the rose garden, over there are the stables. We command about fifty horses," she explained as they walked along the path from her manor.

"Please, madam, can you walk a little slower?" he asked, picking up his pace.

"If you can't keep up with me, don't expect me to accept you into my life. Now, over there—"

He grabbed her arm and whirled her around to face him.

"Katheryn, if you marry me, you'll have everything I own at your disposal. I have ten times the property your father has. Think of the possibilities we can accomplish with both of our estates. We will travel from Africa to the northern shores of England. I will try to make you happy and give you all my love."

"Sir, Viceroy, please let go of my arm," she said, shoving one of his hands away.

He loosened his grip.

"Please tell me you'll consider my offer," he said.

Pulling away from him, "It will be considered. I'm tired," she said and marched back to the castle, leaving the viceroy staring after her swaying jaunt.

Count Gawain watched as his daughter entered through the main doors and run up the stairway. The viceroy followed close behind and approached the count.

"Well?" the count asked.

"She didn't say no. Give her a day or two. We'll become friends and I'll coax her again," Viceroy Edmond assured.

"Ah, come into my study. I need to show you something. Brandy? Tea, for your liking?"

"I'd prefer tea."

"I say, my good friend, I am sure glad you have come," the count said, placing his arm around the viceroy's shoulders.

"Here, I have to show you this, so you understand what is at stake," the count said, leading the viceroy over to the tall chest of drawers.

He lifted up the cloth scarf and withdrew a small dark brown box from the top drawer. The count set the container on a small table in the center of the room. He withdrew an old key from his pocket.

"What is this?" the viceroy asked.

"This, my friend, is what represents our union once you have wed my Katheryn."

The old count placed his gnarled fingers across the latch, inserted the tiny key, and opened the box. In the dim light from the fireplace, the viceroy could see the jeweled neckless sparkle back at him.

"Ah, the Jewel of the Danube. I heard you might have it."

"Yes, and as long as it remains in my possession, no one can challenge me for my lands. Do you see why this marriage is so important to me? Once you wed my daughter, this becomes yours."

"I do, old friend. Continue to keep it under lock and key. Who else knows it is here in your bureau?"

"Katheryn, and now you."

"Thank you for showing the necklace to me."."

The count restored the jewelry to its box. He placed it back into the drawer and covered the handle with the lace scarf.

That evening, everyone filled themselves with venison, pheasant, and sweet breads. Before they retreated to their bedrooms, the viceroy decided to take a walk through the castle hallways. He stopped to admire a painting of a regal woman from the count's family when he heard someone run down the stairs. As he looked over the top of the banister, he thought he witnessed a flash of blue color running out the front door. Shaking his head, he decided it must have been one of the help. Moving on, he headed down the hallway toward his room.

Upon entering, he noticed the warmth from the lit fireplace. His bed made and covered with his mother's quilt. A wash bowl lay on top of a dresser with a face cloth folded nearby. His servant knocked and entered his room.

"Sir, do you desire assistance?" the young man asked.

"No, I'll be fine. Goodnight."

"Yes, sir," his attendant said, backing out of the bedroom.

Chapter 5 - Joyce and Bob

Rosetta's eyes drooped in uncontrolled sleep. Her hands relaxed, letting the book fall to the floor. Dolly barked at the offending item and jumped onto Rosetta's lap.

"Whoa, I guess I fell asleep," she said, catching her breath from the weight of her dog.

Nuzzling her face into the dog's short soft hair, she looked up at the wall clock reading ten to three. "Oh, look at the time. I bet you're hungry." Dolly barked and jumped off her lap.

Rosetta glanced at the list she had written down as to what she needed to do tomorrow. She wanted to make sure her mail stopped, and notify the neighbors to watch her house.

After her ex-husband left, she tore out all the wires connecting the security devices he had installed in a fit of rage. Once she calmed down she returned some of the devices to the hosting company. Others were nonreturnable until their contract ran out.

She rose out of her chair and made a half sandwich. She didn't want to eat much as she wanted to go to the church potluck this evening. Afterward, as she and Dolly snuggled down into the sofa to watch a movie on the television, her cell phone rang. Muting the sound of the television with the remote, she noticed Mr. Heyburn's name on the screen.

"Hello, Mr. Heyburn, yes we are almost packed and ready to go. No problems are there?"

"Rosetta, I want to wish you a safe journey and enjoy your trip," her boss said.

"Well, thank you. I'll see you in two weeks," she said.

"Yes, don't worry about things here. Goodbye."

"Goodbye," Rosetta said and hung up her cell phone.

Dolly ran up to her. *"Now, wasn't that an interesting call."* She thought. *"My boss is a busy man. Why would he call me? I'm thinking this too much. He just wants to make sure I'm okay with my trip."*

Rosetta brushed off the odd feeling as she entered her bedroom when her cell phone rang again. This time it was her ex-husband.

"Oh, hi, Stan," she sighed with restraint.

"Hello, Rosetta. I thought I'd call and see if we can get together sometime."

"Stan, don't call me on some pretense. What do you really want?" Rosetta asked.

"I'd rather I talk to you in person."

"That means you either want to borrow some money from me or you're—you're getting married again aren't you?"

She knew this might happen but hadn't thought about it for some time. She loved Stan and this would put a little stab into her heart. She waited for his answer.

"Well…"

"You have one more year to pay for Joyce's tuition. Other than that, you can do what you want."

"It would mean a great deal for me to have you and the children at my wedding," Stan said.

She loved Stan and this put a little stab into her heart. She waited for his answer.

"You have to be kidding. I can't speak for your grown children. You'd have to ask them."

"I was hoping we could have at least a family dinner together."

"You've set your hopes too high. I have things to do. Goodbye, Stan," Rosetta said and hung up on him.

Rosetta shook her head to rid her brain of the toxin she felt migrating into her thoughts. Once her divorce was final, she made Stan remove the rest of the surveillance devices on the roof he had installed. Weeks later, she spotted one of the cameras mounted in her fichus tree, still operating. She felt he couldn't be trusted during the divorce proceedings.

She looked down at Dolly and picked the terrier up into her arms. Noting the time on her watch, she decided to run next door to give her neighbor an extra key to the house. Holding the key was one thing, but she didn't want Martha Tennison to watch Dolly. The last time she did, her dog got out of the fenced in yard and everyone on her block spent all day out searching. Martha would do anything for her neighbors but sometimes her memory fails her.

She hurried up the front sidewalk and up the steps of her neighbor's house. Martha answered her door.

"Oh, hi Rosetta. What brings you out on a cold day today?" Martha asked.

"I brought you my house key in case of an emergency. I'm going to be gone for two weeks."

"All right. Where will you be going?"

"I'm going to Europe with my daughter, Joyce."

"That sounds exciting. Well, you two have fun," Martha said.

"We will," Rosetta said.

"Oh, what about your dog?"

"She's taken care of. My son will take her tomorrow to his house."

Rosetta turned and waved.

"Thanks again, Martha."

"Bye."

Rosetta walked back to her house. She dressed for the church potluck social this evening and fed Dolly her evening bowl of kibble. She poured two cans of sliced peaches into a bowl and called it her donation to the church meal. She left the dog chowing down and snuck out of the back door to drive down to the church.

On Wednesday morning, Rosetta worked on repacking her luggage and carry-on bag in the bedroom. She added a few more blouses to her suitcase. Dolly jumped on the bed and sniffed her open baggage.

When the front doorbell rang, Rosetta put her things into the suitcase.

"That might be Bob," she said to the dog.

Dolly followed her down the hallway and began barking.

"Shush, and stay put," she ordered the terrier.

Opening the front door, she welcomed in her son, Bob.

"Oh, come in. I'm so glad you are taking care of Dolly," she said with open arms.

Bob hugged her back, smiling at his mother.

"Sit down, would you like some coffee?" Rosetta asked.

"Thanks, Mom. I will. Come here you hound" he said to the dog and rubbed the back of Dolly's head. He looked around the room and spotted the coffee pot set on the center coffee table. He picked up a cup and poured himself the hot brew into the mug.

"Joyce not here yet?"

"She's coming. She has a late work shift today and we have a hair appointment later today. How are the children?"

"Good. They are excited that they get to have Dolly over. I've been putting off getting them a dog for now."

"Oh, do go to the pound when you decide or the Humane Society."

"We will. I'll go to the Humane Society. They have private patrons taking care of the animals. I know someone involved. They don't euthanize after a time period like the pound does. So tell me about your trip. Two weeks?"

"Yes, from Budapest to Amsterdam, The Grand European Tour," she said, spreading her hands into the air.

"I know you and Joyce will have fun. Take lots of pictures for us," Bob said, scratching Dolly's ears.

"Oh, I will."

The front doorbell rang.

"That must be Joyce. Why don't you see if she needs any help with her luggage?"

Rosetta opened the front door and noticed her daughter had only a medium sized suitcase.

"Is this all you're taking?" she asked.

Joyce walked in and spotted her brother.

"Yes, it is and my carry-on bag. I like to travel light," Joyce replied.

"Now I feel overpacked," Rosetta said. "Maybe you can help me leave some things here."

When Bob stood up, he set his half drank coffee cup on a coaster on the low table.

"Where's your kennel for Dolly. I have to leave and head back to work," he asked.

"It's over here by the sofa. She likes to sit in it when I'm cleaning the house. I believe she thinks it's her inner sanctum sanctorum."

"That's funny, Mom," Joyce said.

"Then she'll be just fine. We'll take good care of her," Bob said, reaching for the container with the slot holes on the sides.

"Just don't overfeed her. I'd hate to put her on a diet when I return," Rosetta commented.

Bob placed the open kennel in the center of the living room. Dolly, without a command, walked right in. When Bob fastened the small gate on the plastic container, Rosetta's dog began whining.

Bob picked up the kennel and Rosetta placed her fingers through the bars of the latched gate.

"Now, you be good and I'll see you in a couple of weeks. Bye bye," Rosetta said to her dog.

Bob placed a dry kiss against his mother's cheek. He turned and headed for the front door.

"Have a good trip, you two," he said, looking back at them.

Rosetta watched as her son placed Dolly in the back seat of his car. He wrapped the seat belt around it, and wave back to them before he entered the driver's seat. She and Joyce waved back and watched him drive off.

"Okay, Mom, let's see what you can do without in your suitcase. You can buy stuff in Europe if you need anything," Joyce said.

"I know. Drop your suitcase in your old room first. I moved a few storage items out of the way yesterday. Our hair appointments are at three. We have time," Rosetta said.

Joyce ascended the stairs first to pull her suitcase up the steps while Rosetta pushed on the bottom of the luggage. Joyce's room was the first door on the right.

"Yes, I can see I have just enough room to lie down," Joyce said, smiling as she stared at the stacks of storage boxes around her old bed.

She pushed her rolling suitcase inside and left it against the door. Then she followed her mother into the master bedroom. On the bed, the open luggage yawned before them. Joyce checked through her mother's items and made an assessment.

"If you take just three or four blouses, two skirts, and maybe two pairs of slacks you would have room to bring back souvenirs," she said.

"Only four blouses for fourteen, I mean sixteen days?"

"You don't have to wear them in a row, just alternate them. If you have any worn underwear, bring those. You can trash them later so they won't take up space returning home. And remember the boat has laundry service."

Rosetta stared at her open suitcase and smiled at her daughter.

"I'm so glad you are coming with me. This will be fun," Rosetta beamed.

"I'm excited too. Say, what are your gloves doing in here?" Joyce asked.

"Sometimes my hands get cold. Since they don't take up much room, I'll leave them there. You never know when you'll need a pair of gloves," Rosetta said.

"Suit yourself."

"We should leave for our appointments. It's almost two thirty. I miss Dolly already," Rosetta said, glancing around the bedroom.

They left in Joyce's car and arrived at the hair salon for their haircuts.

"You want to what?" the stylist asked Rosetta.

Rosetta always had long hair and came into the salon just for a shampoo and a trim. This was the most dramatic style she would receive since Joyce was born.

"I want my hair cut short like my daughter's. Donate it to one of those charities you sponsor.

"Yes, ma'am," the stylist said and opened her station drawer to bring out her sharp scissors.

After they returned home, Joyce pulled out the spaghetti bag for dinner. Rosetta already had a boiling pot going on the stove.

"I feel a little naked without all of my hair in the back," Rosetta said, spreading her fingers across the back of her neck.

She opened the plastic bag, stacked the spaghetti sticks into the boiling water, and added a pat of butter.

"You look younger, Mom," Joyce said as she pulled an unopened jar of spaghetti sauce out of the cupboard.

"Nothing biased here," she replied, moving to her cutting board to dice some onions for the meatballs.

"You know there is a lot of walking on the tours we signed up for. You might even lose a few pounds," Joyce said.

"Are you telling me something?"

"I like you the way are, but heart attacks are common for your age bracket. I just want you around long enough to see your second set of grandchildren," Joyce said, smiling.

"I'll take that as a suggestion. Are you seeing anyone? There are some lettuce and carrots in the fridge. You can make us a salad," Rosetta said.

Joyce smiled again. "Not at the moment, but one has to think of the future, right?"

"All right, I won't ask until you're ready," Rosetta said as she pulled the bowl of thawed hamburger out of the microwave. She added the chopped onions and oats. After she mixed the meat well, she rolled individual meatballs and one at a time placed them into her fry pan with a little olive oil.

Stirring the boiling water containing the loose spaghetti, she checked to make sure the strands weren't sticking to the bottom of the pot. Rosetta bent down to one of the lower cupboards and pulled out a strainer for the noodles.

Joyce flipped the meatballs. She opened the cupboard with the dishes and pulled out two large dinner plates. Then she picked out two glasses off the shelf.

"Do you want water with dinner or coffee?" Joyce asked.

"No coffee for me in the evening. I want to sleep. Water is just fine," Rosetta replied.

Rosetta and Joyce rose early the next morning on Thursday and made sure their tickets were secure in their carry-ons. Their flight took off at noon, but they wanted to check in early, just to make sure they wouldn't have to rush.

After loading Joyce's car trunk with their suitcases and carry-ons, they locked up the house. Driving away, Rosetta looked back at her darkened home and sighed.

"Feeling relaxed already?" Joyce asked, turning onto the main road to the freeway.

"Not until we are on the plane. Then I'll worry about it landing. You know me," Rosetta said.

"Yes, mother, I do."

Chapter 6 – Across the Ocean

Over eight hours of flight can make most people irritable, but with the large selection of movies to choose from, the three meals and a snack to eat, the two women had lots to talk about and keep themselves occupied.

"What did your boss say when you asked to go on this trip?" Joyce asked.

"He was very encouraging. He even suggested I take one of the new employees. That's why I was so glad you said you'd come with me. That woman didn't seem to know how to behave in an office. Then, of course, the tickets had been paid for."

"I'm glad things worked out this way. Well, I'm going to the restroom," Joyce said and rose out of her aisle seat.

Rosetta, sitting in the center of the three-seat row, nodded and pulled out her digital reader. She had bought and downloaded the book she was reading at home to keep the weight down in her bag. As soon as she saw her daughter walking toward her in the aisle, she unbuckled and struggled out of the cramped row of seats from the center.

"I need a walk too," she told her daughter when she returned.

Joyce sat in the center seat and placed Rosetta's reader in the aisle seat. This would allow her mother to get in and out of the row easier. After some time had passed, her mother returned.

When Rosetta returned she noticed Joyce had changed seats with her.

"Oh, thank you. I had a hard time getting out of that center one," Rosetta said, picking up her reader from the cushion.

"You were gone a long time. Is everything okay?" Joyce asked.

"Yes, I just stopped to talk to one of the stewardess's and she—that one over there," Rosetta said, pointing across the rows of occupied seats. "—and she is from England."

Settling in once more, Rosetta was about to turn on her reader when a man walking through the aisle, bent down to look at her.

Dressed in a loose gray street suit, he wore a black ball cap low over his eyes. Rosetta, startled, looked up at him. He had one hand crossed over his waist behind the loose edge of his blazer.

"Oh, I'm sorry, ma'am. I thought you were someone else. Have a good trip," he said and continued walking down the aisle.

"Well, that was weird," Joyce said.

"Yes, I don't think I look like most people," Rosetta said.

"Well, you know what they say, we could have a twin somewhere in the world. Bob once told me he thought he saw me at a festival I've never been to."

"What movie are you watching?" Rosetta asked, pointing at the monitor screen embedded into the seat in front of them.

"I don't remember—some comedy."

"Maybe I'll just take a snooze. I can't seem to keep my eyes open. We'll lose a whole day by the time we land."

"Here, I already undid my blanket pack, you can use it if you want to," Joyce offered, passing hers over.

Rosetta took the navy blue blanket and laid it over her chest. She reclined the seat a couple of inches and closed her eyes.

The man in the gray suit sat down next to his friend in the rear of the plane.

"I don't understand. I thought he would be taking this flight," he said, buckling his seat belt.

"Maybe he canceled or missed it. Wish we could use our phones here," said the other man.

"We'll call as soon as we land. Got four more hours," said the gray suit, pointing at his wristwatch.

Rosetta murmured something and turned her sleeping head to one side. Joyce pulled up the blue blanket around her mother's shoulders.

A knight on a white horse rattled across the wooden bridge. A young woman in a light blue flowing dress waved at him as he charged his enemy on the other bank of the river. The horse's hooves beat louder and louder on the slats of timber—

The food cart bumped Rosetta's seat. The abrupt awakening startled her. She sat upright and noticed the blanket Joyce had given her now draped around her knees.

"Sorry, ma'am, which dinner do you want?" the steward asked, bringing Rosetta to reality.

"Oh, uh, the turkey dinner, and a coke, please," she replied, desiring to increase her alertness.

"I'll have the turkey one as well," Joyce said.

The passenger next to the window was asleep. Joyce nudged him. In his forties, he wore a dark blue suit and headphones.

"Sir, do you want dinner?" Joyce asked.

"Huh? Oh, yes," he muttered, taking his headphones off.

"Turkey or beef, sir?" the steward asked again.

"Beef is fine," he murmured.

Receiving the meal from the steward's outstretched hand the man leaned toward Joyce. "Thanks, I would have slept through that. I did one time and by the time I got up to get one from them, they were out."

"No problem," Joyce said. She turned toward her mother who had unwrapped her meal. "How is it?"

"Good, or I'm starving. Didn't we just have a snack a couple of hours ago?"

"Mom, there's that man again," Joyce said, nodding toward the gray-suited passenger as he talked to a steward. Rosetta noticed he finished his conversation and headed in their direction. He approached their row of seats and stopped.

"I'm sorry to bother you again, ma'am, but I was hoping to locate a friend of mine on this flight. Was your ticket a missed flight by someone else?" he said.

"No, not missed. Maybe he'll be on the next flight," Rosetta replied, giving him her courtesy smile.

She stabbed another piece out of her turkey dinner.

"Yes, thank you," he said and continued his walk to the rear of the plane.

"Mom, why didn't you tell him, the man died and we got his tickets?" Joyce asked, finishing her baked turkey.

"Because the newspaper said the man who died had been in trouble with the police. I didn't want this guy to think we were associated somehow. He looks unsavory to me. Oh, look, a chocolate chip cookie," Rosetta said, pulling the confection from the small food box.

"Yes, he does. I'm going to save my cookie. I'm stuffed," Joyce said, pushing her wrapped treat into her pants pocket.

"Here take mine. I can't eat another bite. I read on the menu we'll get a breakfast sandwich before we land."

The steward came by with the garbage sack. Rosetta, Joyce, and the other passenger next to the window passed their trash to the aisle.

"Are you going to sleep some more?" Joyce asked.

"No, I'm too wide awake now. You take this blanket," Rosetta offered, holding an end up for Joyce to grab.

Joyce folded up her tray, locked it in place, and then pulled the blanket over her chest. "I'm going to try and take a nap," she said, wrapping the blanket around her shoulders.

"Maybe I'll fill out these postcards to my friends," Rosetta said, also folding up her tray in the seat back before her.

She up righted her chair back and reached for her carry on under the seat in front of her. Before she realized the time, she killed two hours writing her postcards, watching a comedy show on the small video screen, and making notes in a small journal. Before the next mealtime arrived, she pulled out her electronic reader and read more from her book.

Sleep overcame the viceroy until he heard voices shouting. He pulled his long robe over his bedclothes.

Opening his door a few inches, he tried to ascertain what was going on.

"Where have you been?" he heard the count shout from the main floor below.

Then Henry heard a woman crying. "Oh, you'll never understand, father. I'm going to bed."

"That's where you should be," the count said, raising his pointed finger into the air.

Watching from his lofty position, Henry witnessed Katheryn in her blue riding attire running upstairs to her room at the end of the hall. *"Where had she been?"* he asked himself. Sighing, he closed his door and walked over to his window. Down in the courtyard, he caught a glimpse of a dark horse's rear galloping away. The moonless night outside prevented him from identifying the rider. *"Who was that horsemen? Was Katheryn seeing someone at this hour?"* he asked himself. Drawing the heavy velvet curtains closed, he knew dawn would be long in coming. He removed his robe and slid into the feathered bed.

As he slept, the viceroy rolled over when a bump hit against the thick walls followed by a muffled yell...

The food cart rolled by again with the breakfast choices an hour before their plane would land.

"I don't know if I can eat another bite. Our seatmate is asleep again," Joyce said, looking to her left.

"I'll just get one for the both of us and him," Rosetta said.

When the steward stopped by with breakfast, Rosetta ate the fruit cup and half of her sandwich. Joyce placed her wrapped sandwich in her carry-on tote and offered the rest of her meal items to the awakened passenger sitting next to her. He thanked her and finished them off.

Over two thousand miles away the New York City police finished their investigation in Harry's apartment and pulled off the caution tape across the door in the hallway. Forensics already had removed the body a few days ago, and the officers took away the numbered yellow sign tabs from the floor.

Mr. Alverez, the landlord, stood in the hallway. He approached one of the officers leaving the crime scene. For several days, the police had been in and out of the apartment and he needed to rent the room.

"Can I rent the room out now?" he asked the officer at the top of the stairway.

"Yes, but our cleanup didn't remove the stain in the carpet. You should replace it," the officer said and walked away.

The landlord watched the officer step down the stairs until he headed out of the front door. Alvarez pressed his lips together and walked inside to look around the room before he locked the apartment door. Staring at the large bloodstain on the carpet, he noticed the brown couch needed replacing as well. When he left the apartment, he set the code over the knob to lock the door and then walked back downstairs. As soon as the hallway cleared, a shadow edged around a corner and moved closer to the door. The figure peered over the railing and made sure Mr. Alverez would not return, for now.

Glancing in both directions, the figure's black-gloved hands pulled out an electronic radio-frequency identification

(RFID) device. He removed a blank key card from his pocket and recorded the code from the lock onto the card. He waved the card over the lock. As soon as he heard the catch released, he darted inside the apartment.

Once inside, he latched the door behind him. Everything looked neat and in its place until he noticed several envelopes stacked on a nearby desk. Sifting through them, he came across a bulky piece of mail to the former occupant.

Tearing it open, he found five handwritten sheets on weathered notepaper with torn edges. Stuffing them back into the envelope, the intruder slipped it into his jacket and unlocked the door. He peeked in both directions into the hallway. With no one in sight, he stepped into the hallway, closed the door behind him, and then ran to the building's back exit stairwell.

Once inside his car, he took off his hat and gloves. The man pulled out his cell phone and called his contact.

"Yes, I have them. Good. I'll see you in two weeks," he said, disconnecting the line.

Peering down the street behind his car, he pulled away from the curb and disappeared into the heavy traffic.

Chapter 7 - Amsterdam

Rosetta's plane made a smooth landing in Amsterdam with just a slight bump before it taxied toward the terminal. Large vehicles latched onto the nose of the aircraft, guiding the airplane near the terminal's entrance doors. As hundreds of people filed off the plane, they walked into a large room. Rosetta glanced over the disembarking passenger heads, trying to determine where to find their larger suitcases which should be coming off the airplane. Many hotel people in the receiving area held up location signs to attract their guests.

"Mom, I see a restroom sign over there. You go and I'll watch for our driver's sign. Leave your carry-on with me," Joyce suggested.

"Okay, I won't be long."

When Rosetta returned, she traded places with her daughter.

"I haven't seen our hotel sign or our bags, yet," Joyce said.

"Use the restroom and I'll see where all these people are going. I'll meet you back here next to this trash can," Rosetta said.

She observed her daughter's fading stature merging into the crowd of passengers. Rosetta rolled both carry-ons over to the exit. She didn't want to go through just yet because she would not be able to return and locate Joyce. There in the other room, she could see a bearded man holding their hotel sign. She waved but he hadn't noticed her.

Just then her airline seatmate walked by.

"Sir," she said, getting his attention. "Would you mind letting that man over there with the Highlander sign know we are here? The name is Blessing," she asked.

"Sure," he said and walked through the exit arch.

She waved when the passenger notified the sign holder. Their greeter smiled and waved back. She hurried back across the room to find Joyce. Her daughter stood near their meeting spot. Rosetta waved and gestured her to come.

"He's outside, here's your bag," Rosetta said, passing the pullout handle toward her daughter. She walked toward the exit with Joyce right behind her. Rosetta approached the man with their hotel sign and gave him their names.

"I have your suitcases right here, madam. Follow me," he said and pulled their luggage behind his back as he walked.

From the corner of her eye, she noticed the gray-suited man and his partner from the plane as they followed them through the revolving doors. She hurried her pace as the man's friend summoned a taxi when they approach the hotel van.

Their guide escorted Rosetta and Joyce to an open sliding door of the vehicle and loaded their suitcases and carry-ons in the rear of the van. They ducked their heads as they climbed on board behind the driver's seat. After starting the engine, their driver drove away from the airport terminal. Rosetta looked behind and noticed the gray-suited man entered a taxi. She couldn't help wonder why he was following them.

"Ah, you are visiting our great city?" their driver asked as he approached the highway, heading into the city.

"Yes, we are taking a river trip. Is it always this humid here?" Rosetta asked, breathing in the warm moist air.

"Only during summer. It's hotter than usual this year," he said. "Staying in Amsterdam long?"

"Just tomorrow. Today we sleep," Rosetta commented.

"Yes, it was a long flight," Joyce added.

The driver drove to the rear of the hotel and pulled out their luggage from the back. Rosetta handed him two American dollars as a taxi pulled up next to the curb behind them.

"You do take U.S. money, don't you?" she asked.

"Yes, all kinds of money. Best you buy euros for shopping on your trip," he advised.

They thanked him and walked into an opened foyer. There they approached two elevators. Joyce pushed the single button between them. When an elevator door opened, they pulled their luggage inside the compartment. Joyce pushed a button that said Lobby in English. She noticed the gray-suited man and his friend had just stepped into the foyer as the doors closed.

When the elevator stopped, the inside doors behind them slid apart. A woman in a red uniform greeted them and directed them to the reservation desk up five steps in the rear of the room.

As they pulled their luggage around the corner, Joyce spotted the reservation desk as daylight streamed in through the front doors. Rosetta proceeded to check in while Joyce waved over a bellhop. The porter brought out a luggage carrier and then loaded their bags onto the platform. Joyce gave him the room number before he pushed the cart into the next open elevator.

After receiving her hotel tour confirmation for tomorrow from the desk clerk, Rosetta looked around the lobby. She didn't see the gray-suited man from the airplane.

"Let's sit over there and rest a bit. I'm bushed already," she said, gesturing to the collection of upholstered chairs and fireplace.

Rosetta plopped her large frame into the soft chair. She had never felt this exhausted. Joyce did as well and pulled out their schedule.

"Oh, there's the place we can eat breakfast. We'll have to rise early. Our tour tomorrow begins at nine," Joyce said, reading the itinerary.

"I'm recovered. Are you ready to head for our room?" Rosetta asked.

"Yes, lead the way. Mom. I'm ready to take a shower."

They rode the elevator to the third floor and counted the room numbers down the hallway. They passed several suitcases delivered outside the rooms for their owners. Rosetta spotted hers and checked their room number. Joyce waved her room card and unlocked the door.

They pulled in their luggage, locked their door, and ran to their beds. Joyce flung herself onto one of the two queen beds which filled the room space. Rosetta sat down on the other bed and lied down.

Lying flat on their backs, Rosetta said, "I don't think I can get up."

"I can't either, but I'll try," Joyce giggled.

The next morning, they packed one of the hotel totes provided in their room with bottled water for their day tour. Rosetta and Joyce carried their passports in a small clutch they wore under their blouses. Rosetta pulled out a couple of expandable sunhats from her suitcase while Joyce looked out of their room window over the city buildings.

"Oh, look, Mom, doesn't the city look great?"

"Yes, it does. Our itinerary says to meet in the rear lobby. That must have been where we entered yesterday. Let's head down now and eat breakfast. Do you have your passport with you?"

"Yes, Mom, I have it right here," she said patting her chest. "Is your camera in your tote?"

They smiled at their mother and daughter check on each other. As they stepped outside of their room door, Rosetta noticed several people also leaving their rooms.

"Maybe they will be our tour mates," she said.

"Oh, Mom, this is so exciting. We are in a foreign country," Joyce said, grinning and clapping her hands.

Rosetta smiled at the little girl she remembered.

"This is fun. I'm glad you came with me."

Locating the dining room, they walked in and saw the hotel had set up a buffet for the morning meal.

Their bus held close to forty people from all over the world. Rosetta struck up a conversation with an American couple across the aisle. She could tell when they conversed in a western accent. The woman was slight in stature like Joyce with dark hair and the husband had straight white hair.

"Is this your first time here?" the lady asked.

"Yes, my family came from Denmark. I'm excited about seeing what the land looks like," Rosetta said. "How about you?"

"We're from Arizona," the woman said.

Their bus driver closed the bus door and pulled out into traffic.

"It's our second time. My grandmother and her nine children came over before the second world war," the lady said. "She brought them over by ship from Europe, twice traveling in in steerage."

"Those trips must have been rough back then. We wouldn't be able to travel that way today. She wasn't traveling with a husband at the time?" Rosetta asked.

"No, there's no record of him until my cousin did some research. He thinks he found our grandfather on a census in South Africa. I guess he traveled around a lot. Someday, I'll have to visit there."

Their bus stopped for a street light.

"Oh, look at that, Mom—bicycles, hundreds of them parked in that storage garage."

"And look, there are three signal lights on the sidewalk. One for the cars, one for the bikes, and one for the pedestrians," Rosetta commented.

The lady across the aisle spoke, "Yes, Amsterdam and Colone are well known for accommodating bicyclists. It's too expensive to drive a car here."

"How much is the gas here?" Rosetta asked.

"Six to ten of our dollars a gallon," the woman replied.

Rosetta gasped. "I had no idea people paid that high over here."

Rosetta slung her camera case strap over her shoulder while Joyce carried their tote with their bottles of water. They both wore their tour receivers around their necks. Their guide recited the history of Amsterdam as they walked past fresh food vendors and souvenir stands. She allowed the passengers some free time to visit one of many the gift shops surrounding the plaza. Rosetta and Joyce headed for one shop with a postcard stand outside near the open door.

"I just want a magnet. I have so much stuff at home, I don't need any more bulky items," Rosetta said and headed for the display along the wall.

Choosing the one she wanted, she paid the clerk in Euros and dropped her souvenir into their tote bag. Stopping at a small grocery store, they each bought a soda pop and continued their way back to their bus. As they passed a vegetable stand, a young boy ran by and bumped Joyce. A second boy, racing after the first one, pulled the tote from Joyce's shoulder.

"Hey!" Joyce shouted.

The second boy with the tote caught up with the first youngster. They both disappeared behind the line of buses.

"Well, can you beat that? Are you all right, Joyce?" Rosetta asked, turning toward her.

The white-haired man they had met earlier on the bus stopped to help them.

"Are you ladies okay?" he asked.

"Well, we're a little upset but fine. We had nothing of value in the tote. Oh, except my magnet. There's our guide I'll ask her if I can run back and get another one."

"Hurry, Mom,"

Once Rosetta got the go-ahead from her guide, she trotted back to the gift shop. After a few minutes, she climbed into the bus. Searching through the crowded bus as to where Joyce sat, she located the empty seat next to her daughter.

"Tell me, you aren't hurt from that, are you? That would have wrenched my shoulder good," Rosetta asked.

"No, I'm fine, just a little rattled," Joyce assured.

They marveled once again at the city's buildings along the streets their bus traveled. Rosetta noticed the shoppers dressed just like people did back home in the states. *"We're the same the world over,"* she thought. Once back in their hotel, Joyce let her mother take a shower first.

"Looks like we don't have to catch our plane to Budapest until eleven in the morning," Joyce remarked. Scrolling through her phone, she looked over her schedule.

"Good, we can sleep in a little," Rosetta said and headed for the bathroom and the tub.

Later they packed what they didn't need right away into their suitcases. Per instructions from the hotel, they set their large suitcases outside their door for a courtesy pickup to their next flight.

Chapter 8 - Budapest

During the night, Rosetta woke up to sounds of bumping against her hotel room door. Annoyed, she couldn't believe the walls were thin enough to hear through. She always asks for the top floor in motels to avoid rambunctious neighbors above her. Realizing the noise came from their door, she decided to see what was going on.

"Wake up, Joyce. I'm going to check on our bags," she warned.

"Careful, Mom," her daughter muttered, sitting up in her bed.

Rosetta pulled out her robe hanging in the closet. When the bumping sounds ceased, she waited a moment and placed her ear next to the door. Peeking through the peephole, she saw no one. With the lock chain still attached, she opened the door and then peered out into the hall. She gasped. All their things from their suitcases were scattered on the hallway floor.

"Joyce, come here. I need your help," Rosetta called back into the room. Joyce came to the doorway in her bare feet.

"Just a minute and I'll get something on," her daughter said.

Joyce rushed back inside to tie a robe around her night tshirt. They spent the next few minutes picking up their belongings and hauling their luggage back into their room for repacking.

"I'm going to call the front desk," Rosetta said.

"But I don't think they can do anything. Let's just pack and put them back out. I wouldn't think it would happen again, do you?" Joyce asked.

"Okay, but I'm going to call and make sure a bellman picks up the bags."

After they had repacked and set their luggage once again out into the hallway, Rosetta called the hotel desk to complain.

"Yes, I want our luggage picked up right now. You wouldn't believe the mess someone made and I'm not going to stand guard out there all morning. Thank you, I'll be watching for him," Rosetta said to the hotel manager.

"Mom, why don't you go to bed and I'll watch for the bellman," Joyce offered.

"Thank you, hon, what a day. I'm too wired. I think I'll read a bit."

Rosetta turned on her reader and found a comfortable spot to sit at the head of her bed.

Almost asleep, the viceroy heard a couple of bumps against the thick walls and a muffled yell. Thinking this old castle was filled with unusual sounds and noisy servants, he rolled over and fell into a deep sleep.

During the early morning, he awoke to a loud scream ringing outside his door. At first, he laid still wondering if he should be concerned. Deciding the tone of the scream seemed urgent, he jumped out of bed, placing his bare feet on the cold stone floor. He slipped his feet into his wool slippers, grabbed his silk robe off the end of the bed, and whirled it over his shoulders covering his nightdress.

Checking the hallway, he didn't see anything at first in the dim candlelight in the wall sconces. From above, the moon cast its silver glow through a high aperture in the wall toward the first floor. Then, he saw something move. A shadow ran down the stairs. Henry crept into the hallway to look over the banister and saw his friend, the count, lying face up at the bottom of the stairway. The sprawling form on the floor didn't move. The Count's nightgown spread across the decorative rug. The moonlight illuminated his twisted legs as blood seeped from behind his head.

Unable to wrap his mind around the thought his friend could be hurt, or worse, he asked himself, *"Is this some kind of joke?"* At first, he wanted to run downstairs but couldn't bring himself to move. Another high-pitched scream cried out below him. The shocked viceroy watched as the count's daughter ran to her father's bloodied body and knelt beside him. He forced himself to run down the stairs, gripping the handrail as he descended. He found Katheryn sprawled over her father. She looked up at the viceroy. Her white oval face shined in the moonlight as her tears glistened over her round cheeks. The viceroy bent down to her to see if he could help.

Rosetta rose in the morning after six and let her daughter sleep a few minutes longer. She checked outside her door and noted their suitcases were gone. Joyce woke up and stretched.

"The bellman did come, didn't he?" Rosetta asked, turning toward her daughter.

"Yes, and I gave him a tip. I hoped you slept well," Joyce said, stretching her arms out as she yawned.

"I did. I must have fallen asleep reading my book. I had a good dream about the story, but I don't remember it," Rosetta replied.

"That always happens to me. I'll wash up first before we go downstairs for breakfast."

Ready to leave, they took the elevator down to the main floor and entered the dining room. The staff had set the breakfast venue up as a buffet. Rosetta and Joyce found a table in the open seating area. The waiters dressed in their white jackets and black slacks brought the two women their juice and coffee. Rosetta and her daughter found everything they wanted to eat at the buffet tables and returned to their chairs.

Joyce, gazing toward the end of the room where the buffet tables stood, noticed a familiar face.

"Mom, isn't that the man on the plane who wore the gray jacket?"

Rosetta turned halfway in her seat to see where her daughter had pointed.

"I'm not sure at this distance. That man is wearing a brown suit today. Don't attract his attention. Let's just eat and go. We can wait for our transport in the lobby," she said, drinking the last of her juice.

The man never approached them by the time they were ready to leave the dining room. They sat in the lobby until a young lady came over and informed them their ride was ready to take them to the Amsterdam airport.

Their van deposited them off at one of the air terminals. After checking their large suitcases at the airline counter, they rolled their smaller wheeled totes past a long line before Rosetta stopped to ask one of the ticket holders what the line was for.

"You have to go through customs," the young woman said.

They looked back and couldn't see where the line ended.

"Come on, Mom, let's go," Joyce said as she grabbed Rosetta's carry on.

Rosetta walked as fast as she could. Out of breath, they reached the back of the line before ten more people joined them.

"Whew! If I don't lose weight on this trip, I don't know what will," Rosetta exclaimed, still breathing hard.

Rosetta, bored with waiting for the line to move, started a conversation with a redheaded lady just ahead of her and found they were almost neighbors. The woman lived in Maryland. Rosetta worried whether the line will move quick enough for them to make their flights in time.

Before they knew it, they approached the passport-scanning machines. Joyce passed through the scanner first. As Rosetta stepped out to catch up with her daughter, a security guard stopped her.

"I thought I was done," Rosetta said to the official.

"I have to stamp your passport, ma'am," he said.

After he finished his duty, she hurried to catch up to Joyce who had been waiting for her.

"What happened, Mom?"

"Just surprised. He stamped my passport. I never had anyone do that when I came out of Mexico. Scanning is all they require there," Rosetta explained. "Since we don't have to catch our plane to Budapest for two hours, let's sit over here. I see some empty seats." She motioned toward one of the gate seating areas.

"Mom, I'm going to the restroom. Do you want a snack or anything?"

"No, I'm fine. I'll go after you return. Leave your bag with me."

Within a few minutes after Joyce took off, a young man with curly black hair sat down next to Rosetta.

"You speak English?" Rosetta asked, trying to start a conversation.

"No, no English," he replied and opened a newspaper.

Rosetta smiled and nodded as she bent down to locate her reader from her tote. She straightened up and saw he held the paper wide open across his face. Then she felt him bump her carry-on by her feet.

"Sorry, sorry, madam," he said, without moving his newspaper down.

Once he glanced behind his paper as if he were looking for someone. Rosetta assured her carry-on remained zipped, she continued reading.

The dark-haired man jerked to a stand, folded his newspaper, and took off in a trot down the terminal just as Joyce walked over.

"Who was that?" she asked.

"I don't know, but he seemed nervous about something. Of all the places he could sit, he sat down next to me. Said he didn't speak English. How odd. Everyone here speaks English," Rosetta relayed.

"You go to the restroom. I brought some coffee."

"Oh, good," Rosetta said and rose out of her chair. "I won't be long."

As soon as Rosetta returned, Joyce handed her a sealed coffee cup and suggested they sit closer to their gate.

"Good idea," she replied, clutching her coffee cup.

They pulled their carry-on totes two-gate sections further and managed to find empty seats for both of them. Between the anticipation of flying again and all these people around her made her feel nervous.

"Are you okay, Mom?" Joyce asked.

"Yes, how much more time do we have before we board our plane?"

Joyce scanned down her cell phone for her itinerary.

"Another half hour. Oh, there's the time of departure on the wall monitor," she said, pointing.

Fifteen minutes later, the announcement called for disabled and mothers with small children to board their airplane.

"Looks like we are in the back section," Rosetta said, reading her boarding pass. "You'd think they would load the rear of the plane first. Then we wouldn't have a bottleneck trying to squeeze around passengers still loading the overheads."

"I don't know why, either. The airlines must have a good reason," Joyce said. "Okay, they just called our section."

Like cattle through a chute, the airline crew led the passengers outside on the tarmac and loaded one person at a time up to the open jet stairs. Joyce entered the cabin ahead of her mother. This was a smaller plane than the one they took over the Atlantic Ocean and held about fifty

83

people. Joyce found her seat in the middle of the row and Rosetta sat in the aisle seat next to her daughter.

The passengers buckled their seatbelts and waited and waited. A half hour passed when the captain made an announcement.

"Sorry to keep you waiting, ladies and gentlemen. I have to hold my position until I get clearance. There are storms ahead of us and the tower will let us know when it's time to leave," the man's voice said.

"Well, I might as well do some reading. Is it getting hot in here?" Rosetta asked, twisting the vent above her.

Joyce felt the airflow vent above.

"There is some air coming in, but not much. Here, use this," she said, withdrawing a paper hand fan from her purse.

"You think of everything, don't you?" Rosetta asked, accepting the small fan.

"I picked it up at that souvenir shop. A friend of mine was stuck in a plane for two hours before it took off with no air conditioning. I try to prepare for the worst.

Rosetta decided it was too much bother to reach for her carry-on and pulled out the airline magazine from the seat pocket in front of her to read.

After an hour since they boarded, the captain came on and made his second announcement.

"Thank you for your patience. I have been given clearance. We shall leave shortly," he said.

Everyone heard the hatch door slam shut. Then the air conditioning powered on. Rosetta heard many passengers cheer throughout the plane's cabin. Wiping her forehead of sweat, Rosetta bent down to return the magazine.

A. Nation

"Well, that's odd," she muttered, glancing down at her carry-on.

"What's odd?" Joyce asked.

"There's a piece of paper in the side pocket of my tote."

Rosetta pulled out the folded white sheet of paper. She unfolded the note, read it, and then handed the sheet of paper to her daughter.

"Melk Abby? That's it? How did you get this?" Joyce asked, handing the message back to her mother.

"I don't know. I bet that young man put it there but I didn't see him do it. Don't we tour that place on one of our sailing days?"

"Let me check," Joyce said as she scrolled through her cell phone. "Yes, we do. Ooo, I love a mystery. Was the man handsome?"

"I suppose so, a little young for me. He had dark curly hair and since I was sitting down, I'd guess he might be close to six feet tall."

"You always meet the good looking ones," Joyce said.

Their plane took off, allowing the powerful inertial force to push the passengers back into their seats. Once the airplane lifted into the air and leveled, the seat belt symbol above them turned off. Rosetta pulled out her tablet to read more from her book. Their flight to Budapest would take another two hours.

Henry guided the daughter of his deceased friend to a nearby chair. He returned to the body, took off his robe, and covered his friend's death mask.

"I will arrange everything. Will you be all right until I return?" he asked.

85

Her pale face looked at him. "How could this have happened? Did he fall? What will I do now?" she asked, sobbing.

He waited a moment as she cried her sorrow into a whimpered.

"I am here for you. Please remain calm. I'll summon the servants to help. I'll return as soon as I can," he said, holding her hand.

Drawing her handkerchief to her eyes, Katheryn nodded. When she settled a bit, he took off to change his clothes before summoning the house staff.

Still dressed in his bedclothes, he hurried out of the foyer to summon his footman and driver to assist in removing the body.

He glanced at Katheryn who had stopped crying. She sat still, staring straight ahead at the covered white and maroon mound on the floor before her.

Returning with his aides, he saw the count's two male domestics standing around the count's body. He waved the four men to take the body out and have the floor cleaned. They rolled the soiled rug around the count's body and hauled it out of the room.

Assured they would take care of the situation, he ran upstairs and slipped into his trousers. Replacing the bed dress with his day blouse, he washed his face from the basin provided on top of the low cabinetry near the door. All this time, he wondered if the count really did slip down the stairs and fall, or was he pushed.

Running back down the stairs, he noted Katheryn no longer sat in the room. *"Maybe she returned to her bedroom,"* he thought as he rushed upstairs and knocked on Katheryn's door.

"Katheryn, are you there?" he called out.

A few moments of silence passed until he heard the door unlatch and open.

"Henry, is he still—?" she asked. Tear stains draped her plump cheeks.

"No, the servants have removed him. I can call the housekeeper to stay with you," he said.

"No, I'm fine."

Then she flung herself at him, wrapping her arms around his chest. "Oh Henry, I was angry at him when I talked to him last. I feel responsible."

"No, you aren't. I believe he fell. It was an accident," he said, guessing at the possibility.

She raised her head up and a look of horror crossed her face.

"The necklace, we must check the necklace," she blurted out.

"Come with me. We'll check it together," he said and reached for her hand.

They hurried down the stairs and entered the count's study. Katheryn ran to the large bureau and gasped. They both looked at the open drawer and Henry checked for the dark brown box.

"It's gone," he said, facing her.

Drawing her palm to her mouth, Katheryn gasped again as she looked down.

"No, it's on the floor—!" she cried.

He spotted the brown box laying open, exposing the maroon cloth from inside. The necklace was missing. As she wept without control, he held her in his arms whispering, "I'll take care of you, my dear. Please, don't worry."

Rosetta, reluctant to stop reading, closed her reader as the pilot made his announcement about landing.

Chapter 9 - Touring

"Attention everyone, we will be landing in Budapest in twenty minutes. Please fasten your seatbelts," the airline steward announced.

Rosetta turned off her reader and set it inside her carry-on. Joyce woke up after a short snooze and sat upright.

"I'll be so glad when we arrive at our hotel so I can wash up," Rosetta said.

"So will I. What hotel are we staying at?" Joyce asked.

"I chose the Highlander. I'm familiar with their chain of hotels. My customers in the travel agency always book through them."

As they walked off the plane into the terminal, a young man with sandy colored hair waved a Highlander sign back and forth. Rosetta approached him and gave their names.

"Oh, I'm sorry ma'am, but I don't see your names on my register," he said, flipping through papers on his clipboard.

Rosetta frowned since she thought her office clerk had corrected the reservation names. Trying not to worry, she explained to their guide what had happened.

"Oh, we might be under a Mr. Brown's name. He died and I claimed the tickets he bought. Here's our reservation number."

"Ah, yes, here it is. I'll make the adjustment. Follow me, please. I will pick up your suitcases," he said. He walked over to the rows of luggage against the wall. When he found theirs, he grabbed the tow handles and pulled them behind him.

Joyce leaned into Rosetta.

"You didn't happen to notice who Mr. Brown was flying with on the original tickets, did you?" she asked as they walked behind their escort.

"No, I didn't. I was so excited when I found out my destination. I didn't think to look at the other name."

They followed their guide to a white hotel van and climbed in. The driver took them all through the city of Budapest.

"This is the most beautiful city you will view in all of Europe," he said, driving through the city streets. "As you see, we have a cosmopolitan here. All nationalities come during the summer to visit us from Europeans to Asians.

"Once we were two cities, Buda and Pest. In 1793, they joined as one city. Ah, here we are," he said.

He drove the van up to the curb in front of the hotel's entrance. Once parked, he jumped out of the driver's seat to unload the their luggage. Receiving her suitcase, Rosetta handed him two American dollars. He accepted the money and gave them some advice.

"For your convenience, you will need to go to the exchange stations and get Hungarian money. We don't use Euros here. Your hotel may accept Euros, but if you try at a souvenir shop, you will be charged three times that in forints."

"Thank you. The shops do accept credit cards, don't they?"

"Yes, some do, but they prefer the local money due to the high processing fees. Thank you and enjoy your stay," he said and hurried back to his driver's seat.

A. Nation

Once the van pulled away, Rosetta and Joyce pulled their luggage through the sliding doors in the front of the hotel. Wood paneling clad the front counters and the walls behind the clerks at their computers. Rosetta checked in at the reception desk, signing her name on the reservation sheet. To their left, they walked to the row of elevators and entered one. Rosetta pressed the fifth-floor button on the panel. Without a sound, the elevator lifted them up to their floor.

As soon as they exited, the man in the gray suit hurried into the elevator and pressed a button on the hallway panel. Inside, Rosetta watched the sliding doors close.

"There's that man again," Joyce said behind her.

"Let's find our room. I'm not going to worry about him," Rosetta said, as the elevator doors slid apart.

They walked down the hallway until they arrived at the door of their room. Joyce inserted her key card to open their hotel door. Rosetta followed close behind. They surveyed the large room containing two queen size beds, a large bath area with a tub, and a great view out their window.

"Mom, look. We can see over the Danube. There's the Parliament house on the other side," she squealed.

"I gather you like our room?" Rosetta asked.

"Yes, oh yes, you are the greatest, Mom," Joyce said, flinging her arms around her mother's shoulders.

"Thank you, Joyce. That's what a mother loves to hear. Let's get unpacked," Rosetta said after Joyce released her.

They placed their folded clothes from their luggage into the drawers under the forty-eight-inch television set in front of the beds.

"I'm taking a shower, and then you can take yours," Joyce said.

"Fine by me," Rosetta replied trying to decide which drawer to lay her clothes.

After their showers, they dressed in lighter clothes. Joyce donned knee-length slacks and a tank top. "I've noticed several tourists wearing lighter clothing. I don't feel I have to wear more," she said.

"You're right. Besides it's warm outside," Rosetta replied, pulling on a loose knee-length skirt and a sleeveless blouse. "Well, I'm getting hungry. Let's go down and see what's for lunch."

"Don't forget to bring your receiver," Rosetta said. "We'll leave for our tour after we have eaten.

"Got it," Joyce said, picking up the device from its charging station and placed it in her pants pocket.

"We can catch the tour bus at one o'clock to take us to the center of the city. From there we'll go on a walking tour," Rosetta read from their touring itinerary.

"Yes, mother, I know. Oh, here comes our waiter," Joyce said, grateful for the interruption.

Rosetta sighed, trying not to mother her daughter too much. *"Maybe that's why she moved out of the house,"* she thought.

The waiter approached them with wine glasses.

"Would madams enjoy our house wine?" he asked.

"Yes, I would, Joyce?" Rosetta replied.

"Okay, but just a little. I'm the designated walker," she joked.

Rosetta started laughing.

"I see you are having a great time in our city already," the waiter said, pouring each of them a half-filled glass.

A. Nation

Rosetta and Joyce tapped their glasses together and sipped their red wine.

Rosetta stopped and left her addressed postcards at the reservation desk before she and her daughter joined ten other tourists on the small bus. They rode across the Danube into the center of the Buda city. Ornate facades and grandiose statues of men on horses or heroes adorned many of the buildings.

"Some of you may think these buildings are churches. I assure you they are not," their guide said from the front passenger seat next to the driver. "They are businesses or governmental buildings."

Their guide pointed out the American Embassy. Uniformed soldiers guarded the fenced grounds at the front gate. The bus traveled on and soon pulled over to the side of the curb. Once again everyone turned on their receivers hung around their necks by lanyards and touched it to the guide's transmitting paddle as they exited the bus. Rosetta and Joyce inserted the connecting earbuds to hear their guide describe their surroundings.

First, they walked through a farmer's market and on to an open park. In the center of the square was a bronze statue of former President Ronald Reagan. Joyce stood near the statue, while Rosetta took her picture hugging the presidential likeness.

The guide allowed everyone fifteen minutes to shop at the various souvenir stores surrounding the square. Rosetta located a money exchange window and stepped into the small cubicle. She returned with two hundred and eighty-two forints worth a hundred dollars in U.S. money.

"Now we can shop," she declared.

"I see a couple of souvenir shops across this plaza," Joyce said.

Joyce entered one of the open storefronts. On one side of the doorway, a table displayed stuffed animals. On the other side of the entrance, she noticed a pole of greeting cards jiggling in the light breeze. Most businesses didn't have air conditioning, as their seasonal temperatures aren't as hot in August. However, this season, Europe was suffering from a heat wave. The air was stifling inside the souvenir shop. A small fan by the cashier waved hot air back and forth. Rosetta scouted out the magnets and Joyce found some Christmas ornaments to buy.

At first, Rosetta tried to use her credit card.

The clerk in broken English moved her open hand back and forth to refuse the credit card. "No. Pay forints," the middle-aged woman said.

"No problem," Rosetta said.

She noted the price stickers and handed her a fifteen forints for a 12f marked price tag. The clerk returned Rosetta's change of three small coins. Rosetta thanked the clerk.

"How much are the coins worth?" Joyce asked once they left the gift shop.

"Practically nothing. Here, keep them for souvenirs," she said and dumped the unworthy coins into Joyce's hand.

Looking behind Joyce, Rosetta said, "There's our guide. She's waving from over there."

Rosetta pointed toward the middle of the plaza. As they approached their meeting location, they heard the guide explain a sight high on the building façade through their earbuds.

A. Nation

"If you look up at this building and wait when the clock strikes noon, a carousel display will be activated in the tower," their guide said.

Along with several other tour members they waited until the large clock on the side of the building rang. Above in the tower, a carousel consisting of horse statues and their riders rotated around a center post. Then more mechanical horsemen returned in the opposite direction with tiny swords and knocked the first riders out of their saddles. Rosetta could see the scenario better when she zoomed in with her camera.

"Here, Joyce, look," she said handing the camera over to her daughter.

"Wow, that is impressive."

Once the little moving diorama ceased, their guide waved to escort her troop through the gothic building's arch into a small courtyard. Everyone followed the guide into a local restaurant with statues of pigs wearing chef hats beside the archway. From there, a hostess led them to a section of the restaurant that could accommodate large tour groups. Everyone sat down at a long table. Before they had settled in their chairs, the waitresses served Hungarian goulash.

"Looks like tomato soup with potatoes and beef," Joyce said.

"It's good but a little spicy," Rosetta said, dipping her spoon back into the red liquid.

After their soup, the waitress brought triangles of a confection cake. Everyone took one and enjoyed the powdery sweet dessert. The meal finished, their guide escorted them back to their bus, which after a short ride, dropped them off at the hotel. Inside, one of the clerks at the reservation desk gave each passenger a notice about their luggage transport to their riverboat.

"Mom, we have to set our suitcases outside our door tonight. Do you think that's all right?"

"When I talked to the desk in Amsterdam, he assured me that was a rare event. I'll call and find out when the porters would pick ours up."

Returning to their room, they repacked their suitcases close to the pickup time. When Joyce pulled them out into the hallway, she could see many bellmen loading tourist luggage on their carts.

"They are coming," Joyce called back into the room.

"We have to rise early tomorrow. Our tour after breakfast will take us to the parliament building before we board our riverboat. I'll set my phone alarm."

"I will too," Joyce said, sitting cross-legged on her bed.

The man in the gray suit glanced down the hallway as he talked.

"Yeah, boss, I followed them across the courtyard and into the café, nothing unusual yet. Yeah, I'll let you know. Bye."

Chapter 10 – Melk Abbey

Rosetta and Joyce boarded their bus after breakfast and rode to the Capitol building of Budapest. As their tour bus drove across the monumental Chain Bridge over the Danube River, their driver gave them information through the overhead speakers.

"Attention, everyone," their bus driver said. This Chain Bridge is a symbol of our two cities, Buda and Pest and our Hungarian capital. If you wish later, you can take a walk across it but it is 375 meters long. Please don't walk in the heat of the day."

"It was built by Count Széchenyi. When his father died in Buda, people once used the pontoon bridge, but it was not in service during the winter. For fifty years, he financed the building of the Chain Bridge until the construction in 1849 when the revolution began. Hungarian soldiers were the first to walk across this bridge. The Austrians tried to blow this bridge up, but for some reason, the explosives did not go off. Lucky at that time, but in 1945, the Germans blew up the bridge. Of course, years later, many people rebuilt the Chain Bridge again. Have you noticed the two stone lions at the entrance of the bridge from Pest to Buda? The sculptor forgot to carve the tongues. The story goes, he jumped off this bridge in distress over the mistake."

"Look, Mom, a funicular," Joyce remarked as the bus left the bridge.

"A what?"

"It's like a tram, see how steep it is against the hillside," Joyce said, pointing toward the people mover against the hillside. "That's how people down here traverse up to there."

Traveling through the city, Rosetta and Joyce noticed how modern some of the storefronts looked with ancient stonework above them. The bus rounded a large street square and the bus driver pointed out the buildings adorned with Romanesque reliefs in the A-frames. In the center of the square, several statues of riders on their horses stood motionless in time around a circular plaza.

The bus slowed and parked near the parliament building. As the passengers exited the bus, they tapped their receivers to the guide's large numbered paddle. This turned on the audio and made listening easier as they walked together. They entered one corridor and the members of the tour group gazed at the woodwork and gold trimmings in amazement attached to the walls.

Their guide spoke through their earbuds.

"I'll have to instruct you not to take pictures of the crown in the center hall. Guards, stationed around the crown, carry long sabers and perform their maneuvers. They flip those swords around their shoulders every fifteen minutes. So please don't stand near them or you could get cut. Now, please follow me," she said.

The rooms contained high arched ceilings with gothic religious paintings. The tourists walked into the center of the building covered by a large dome. There, in the center under a square glass display case, laid the Crown of Hungary. Covered in gold lacing, it had a red satin cap inserted into the top. The soldiers held their swords over their shoulders and as soon as the tourists had all filed in, they began their routine of marching around the display case.

Rosetta stopped and sat down on one of the long wooden benches. Joyce noticed and walked back to her.

"Mom, you have to keep up."

"I will, too much walking for me. I'm not used to it. You can go ahead."

She didn't want to worry Joyce about her health. *"As soon as I get home, maybe I'll try to lose weight,"* Rosetta thought.

"Okay, but only for a few minutes," Joyce called back as she walked over to a souvenir stand.

That was all the time Rosetta needed to rest. After watching the soldiers march around the glass case, she soon regained her energy. She hurried outside and saw Joyce with their tour group entering a nearby church.

The tour group moved through the building, while a few people stopped near the pews to say their prayers. Joyce and Rosetta exited into the cobblestone square. Their guide said their bus would arrive in a half hour, giving them time to shop some more.

"I'm going to look through that small church over there," Rosetta said, pointing across the square.

"All right, but after fifteen minutes, I'm coming for you," Joyce warned, cocking her head.

Rosetta noticed her gesture and recalled she used to react in a similar fashion when Joyce was slow getting ready for school.

The walk over the cobblestones to the smaller church seemed tiring. Rosetta hadn't walked this much before and she was exhausted. She blamed it on the hot humidity in the air. Entering through the wooden doors, she noticed the church was empty. Religious paintings adorned the stucco walls on each side of the room. Locating a pew in the rear of the chapel, she sat down and closed her eyes for a moment.

In her sleepy haze, she thought she heard two men arguing. Lifting her eyes lids, she could just make out the scenario playing out before her, like actors in a play. Two men struggled near the archway to her left. Then, as she dozed off again, a man's deep voice woke her from behind the pew where she sat.

"Don't turn around," he said.

She thought she saw a shadow in the peripheral of her vision. When she looked to her right, no person was seen there. Shaking the sleepiness from her head, she thought she heard the church door open and click shut. Awake by now, she looked up and saw Joyce.

"Mom!"

Rosetta jerked in her seat. Turning around, she saw Joyce standing behind her with her arms akimbo.

"I'm sorry. Is our bus ready to leave?" Rosetta asked, glancing around the wooden pews.

"What is it?" Joyce asked, dropping her arms.

"Did you just see someone leave through the doors of this church?" Rosetta asked.

"I did hear someone as I entered. Mom, our bus driver wants to leave. Who were you talking to?" Joyce asked.

Rosetta scanned the empty pews.

"I guess no one. I'm ready. Let's go," she said and pulled her tote straps over her shoulder before standing. Rosetta glanced back again to see if someone was still in the church, but there was no one there.

From the courtyard, their bus brought them to the river's edge of the Danube to board their riverboat for the next fourteen days.

As soon as they entered the main deck, a steward received their names, and another officer directed them down the hallway.

"Looks like we got the second deck," Joyce said, smiling.

"And, that's not all. We have a balcony window," Rosetta said, opening their cabin door to a sun-filled bedroom.

Joyce ran to the open curtains of the balcony and drew them aside. She unlocked the glass door and slid it to her right. Bending over the railing, she looked down toward the front of the boat.

"Come on, Mom. Get a load of this view," she called, gesturing for her mother to hurry.

Rosetta stepped out onto the narrow ledge that held two chairs and a small square table. Looking toward the other shore, she exclaimed, "Wow, I really lucked out on this one, didn't I?"

The husky gray-suited man sat in the hotel lobby with his associate, talking on his cell phone to his employer.

"I checked, boss. Brown wasn't on the plane. Maybe he took another one," he said.

"Who had his ticket?" the voice on the phone asked.

"Some lady with gray hair. What shall we do, boss?" the large man asked.

"Check her out."

"Okay, boss—"

He didn't get a chance to finish as the man on the other line had hung up.

"Come on, Pete. We have to find that woman."

That afternoon, Rosetta and Joyce took the walking tour into the city. They found shops selling embroidered laces and Hungarian dolls, which hung on a thin pole outfitted in traditional dresses. As Rosetta glanced away, across the market square, she thought she noticed the well-dressed man from the airport. He rushed into the crowd and almost knocked over a vendor's table. Within seconds, the local police ran by in his direction.

Rosetta moved out to stand on the edge of the sidewalk with her hands shading her eyes

"What's going on, Mom?" Joyce asked when she stepped out of one of the shops.

"I don't know. The police seemed to be chasing that young man. If I didn't know better, I'd say he looks like the same one that passed me the note in the airport."

"Are you sure it was him?"

"Well, no," she hesitated, "but I'm almost sure. Look, there's our guide."

They hurried over to their bus where most of the people in their tour had congregated. Climbing on board, they were ready to tour Melk Abbey, Austria.

"Can everyone hear me? Good," asked their guide as their bus driver drove away from the curb. "The abbey was founded in 1089 as a monastic school. This was a major site for producing written and musical manuscripts for the church.

"The building suffered a fire in 1297 but it was renovated in the baroque style of the seventeenth century. You will see many of the frescos and small statues covered in real gold on columns and walls. Later in that century, this abbey survived other closures by Emperor Joseph II and throughout the Napoleonic Wars.

"Follow me and remember, no flash photographs, please. The paintings are seven hundred years old and they are sensitive to camera flashes. You may use your camera with the flash turned off."

Rosetta and the rest of her tour group passed by the Leopold Altar with a colorful painted frame above the altar on the wall. The frame consisted of dark wood and gold-leafed vines and adorned with cherubs. Toward the altar in the main sanctuary, the golden pulpit hung high above the parishioners on a corner by the side arch over the altar. Rosetta thought the pulpit resembled a large bank canister one uses at the drive-through banks. This is where the priest would stand when addressing his congregation. On top of the pulpit, gold carvings of cherubs struggled to climb up to a golden cross. The bottom of the pulpit also had figures covered in gold. Each figurine held ornate golden shields.

Everyone gasped as they entered each room due to the opulence expressed. The first room had huge columns with relief statues of saints or past resident priests attached. Religious paintings flowed across the ceiling. In the next room, named the White room, the gray-blue walls set as a background to white decorative reliefs of feathering and cherubs. From this room, the tour group entered the ballroom.

Shimmering crystals hung from large chandeliers, invited everyone to dance. One could almost hear the music of the time. Painted walls of religious figures surrounded the room.

"Oh, Mom, I wish I could have lived back in this century," Joyce said, looking up at the chandeliers in awe.

"I wish you could too. Think of the dress you would wear," Rosetta exclaimed, imagining how beautiful her daughter would look in a long flowing gown. "But you wouldn't be allowed here. You had to be a member of the royalty."

"I know that, but I could dream that I could."

The next room held gold overlays on mirrored walls. The room wasn't large but contained a fireplace. An upholstered bench was the only piece of furniture in the room. The tour group stopped to listen to their guide.

"When members of the royalty came to visit, they brought all their furniture and bedding," Their guide said. "During that era, they used lots of makeup and powdered their faces. If for some reason they stood too close to the fireplace to get warm, their makeup, like today, would come off. Thus came the saying, 'They would lose face,'" their guide said.

Everyone laughed at this little joke and the history behind it. Members of the tour continued to follow their guide into the library. Rows and rows of ancient books lined the walls up to the ceiling. Once again, religious figures played out their scenes in the painted ceiling frescos. Two large world globes stood freestanding on opposite sides of the room. As the tour group moved forward through the next set of doors, Rosetta thought she'd sit a bit and found a straight back chair. The high humidity continued to wear her out. *"I'll just rest my eyes for a few minutes,"* she told herself. No windows adorned this room to preserve the vintage books.

After a short time had passed, she heard a crash. Awakened, she thought she saw a shadow move toward the end of the hall. Then she heard footsteps. As she tried to look down toward the entrance of the room, someone whispered behind her.

"Don't turn around," the accented voice murmured.

Frightened as to what this person might do, she held out her purse. "You can take the money in my wallet. Please, don't hurt me," she said.

A light thud hit the floor to her left. Soft footsteps faded away.

"Hello?" Rosetta asked, looking in both directions of the room. "Is anyone here?"

Receiving no answer, she looked behind her. There on the floor next to her purse lay a small square book tied with a thick string. Glancing around again, she saw no one in the grand room. Picking up the wrapped book, she turned it over and peeked inside. The book had handwritten notations within the yellowed pages. The leather-bound cover appeared old. Rosetta determined it looked like a journal, but she couldn't read the words in this unlit room.

Joyce made an appearance and stood in the archway.

"Mom, there you are. Come on before our tour bus leaves without us."

"Oh! I didn't realize—I have to stop in the gift shop."

"There's no time to shop."

"I'm not shopping. Someone dropped this book and it may belong to their library," Rosetta explained.

"Okay, but let's hurry."

They walked down the corridor and entered the gift shop. Approaching a young girl wearing a red dressed with short black hair behind the register, Rosetta asked, "

"I think someone dropped this. Perhaps it belongs in the library."

The girl lifted her shoulders and the upward palms of her hands and shook her head.

"No English," she said, cocking her head to one side.

"Come on, the guide is waving to us," Joyce urged.

"But—"

"No buts, come on, mother," Joyce insisted, hooking her arm into Rosetta's elbow. "You can turn it in on the boat."

Joyce and Rosetta hurried with their tour members over the thick cobblestones and climbed into the air-conditioned bus.

Within twenty minutes, the driver drove through the city towards their docked riverboat. Settling into their seats, Rosetta placed the small leather-bound book into her tote bag.

Chapter 11 - Ransacked

"All I want to do is take a shower. This hot humidity is killing me," Rosetta exclaimed.

"So do I," Joyce said, noticing the vintage volume. "What is that book?"

"I don't know. Either the handwriting is unreadable or it's in another language other than English. Somebody wanted me to have it, but why?"

Settling back into their seats, they enjoyed the view of the city streets and building façades along the roadway. When their bus parked, they, like everyone else, gathered up their bagged belongings and headed for the gangway into their riverboat. As they entered the main reception deck, they turned in their tour cards.

"Did you ladies have a nice day?" the program director asked, grinning at them.

Rosetta noticed his nametag read Hans Becker. She almost handed him the diary but the urgency of a shower and the fact she wanted to try to read it, caused her to decide to do it later.

"Yes, we did," Joyce said as she followed her mother down the hallway toward their cabin.

"Weren't you going to turn that book into the reservation desk?" Joyce asked, shifting one of her tote bags across her arm.

"Yes, but I want to read more if I can."

Rosetta inserted her room card into the lock and opened the door. There they stopped in shock, taking in the chaos before them. Joyce gasped.

"What happened here? Didn't housekeeping do their job today?" she asked, scanning the disarranged bedding and opened drawers.

"The drawers are pulled out. Housekeeping wouldn't do that. Someone has broken in. You go find Security and I'll stay here until you come back," Rosetta said.

"Okay. I'll hurry," Joyce replied.

Joyce set her tour tote down on the hallway floor beside Rosetta and took off in a run back to the reception desk.

Rosetta watched her for a moment before stepping into the cabin room. She glanced around. *"I can't imagine why anyone would do this,"* she thought, easing back into the hallway to see if her daughter had returned.

Spotting a dark-haired woman in a staff apron ascending the stairs from the lower deck, she decided to quiz her on the condition of their cabin.

"Pardon me, did you clean this room?" Rosetta asked.

The young woman peeked inside, then turned back to Rosetta.

"Yes, madam. I cleaned all of these on this deck while you were on tour. I can't understand this. Shall I do your room again?"

"Wait. My daughter went to bring security over here. After he's done looking, you can help us straighten the room.

Within a few minutes, she saw Joyce and a short stocky man in a khaki uniform heading her way. Joyce pointed toward her mother as she stepped aside to let the man pass.

A. Nation

"You have a problem, madam?" he asked. He had a round face with graying hair over his ears. Rosetta guessed him to be about her age—in his fifties.

"Yes," Rosetta replied and gestured her hand toward the inside of the cabin.

"You did not leave it like this?" he asked, turning toward the women as he stood by the scattered covers of the beds.

"No, we were on a tour and just returned to discover the mess in our room. Housekeeping just informed me she had already made up this room," Rosetta explained. "As you can see the curtains have been jerked away."

"Did you lock your doors before you left?" he asked.

"Yes, we did. Didn't we, Joyce."

"I was on the balcony before we left, but I'm sure I locked the sliding door," she replied.

"Have you noticed anything missing?" the man asked.

"No, let me take a look," Rosetta said, entering the room.

"Please step carefully, Madam," he advised.

"I will," Rosetta said as she peered into the open drawers of the nightstand between their beds. The safe in the closet was unlatched but both she and her daughter had taken their passports with them for the tour.

"Mom, your reader is still here," Joyce said.

"Thank goodness. I'd hate not knowing how the story I'm reading ends. Oh, look, someone ripped the pillowcase," she said, pointing to the slice in the pillow fabric. Pillow stuffing lay scattered all over the bed.

"Careful, Mom, you shouldn't disturb anything," Joyce warned when she noticed her mother edging toward the nightstand.

Rosetta lowered her voice and turned to Joyce, "But look, there's something white sticking out from the bottom of my reader."

"We can look at that later," Joyce said in a low tone.

The officer, now in the room, checked the sliding door to the balcony.

Rosetta turned her back on her nightstand while Joyce checked through the closet, discovering a few items lying on the floor. Rosetta bent her knees for a moment, allowing her hands to reach the edge of the paper behind her from the nightstand. While the officer checked the drapery in front of the balcony, She slipped out the square white paper from under her reader and shoved it into her skirt pocket.

When the security officer turned around, Rosetta announced, "I can't find anything gone. If I discover something missing, I'll let you know."

"Good, I will make a report and check this further for you. I'm so sorry, madam."

"Thank you. Sorry, we couldn't be more help," Joyce said. "Can you guess how they might have come in here?"

"My guess would be through your balcony window. If not, your door may have been ajar enough to them to push it in. But I don't see any damage on the door frames," he said, running his hand up and down the molding. "In the meantime, I'll call my assistant to go over your room for a thorough exam. You'll have to stay out of your room for the time being until we have made our investigation. I'll compensate your drinks in the lounge bar.

"After we are done," continued the boat officer, "I'll call Housekeeping to get your things back in order. Since lunchtime is approaching, we should be finished by the time you return after lunch. So sorry, madam, this has happened to you."

"Thank you. Come on, Joyce, we can wash up in the public restroom," Rosetta offered.

When they gathered up their toted items, the security officer said, "You may leave your bags in the closet if you wish."

Rosetta looked at Joyce who shook her head. Turning toward the officer, Rosetta said, "No, we'll keep them with us, thank you anyway."

"I'm glad you said that," Joyce whispered as they walked down the hallway.

"I didn't want anything to interfere with his work. He has to examine the room as we found it."

After washing up the best they could in the public restroom near the reservation desk, they headed for the lounge.

"I'd love a margarita," Rosetta said as they climbed the stairs to the next floor.

"It will cost you between meals," Joyce said.

"Remember, the security man said he's compensating us," Rosetta replied.

They set their totes on a nearby divan by one of the large picture windows before pausing at the bar to order their drinks. Rosetta held out her room key for the bartender to swipe for the boat's records.

"There is no charge for your drinks, madam," he said.

"Then I'll have a lemonade," Joyce ordered.

"Let's sit outside under the canopy," Rosetta said, pointing to one of the tables outside.

"Madam, I can bring your drinks to you," the bartender said.

"Good. We'll be outside on the bow," Rosetta commented.

They gathered up their totes over their arms. Then they walked through the open sliding glass door that separated the lounge from the patio outside. A few people sat at a table on the starboard side of the bow. Rosetta and Joyce stopped at an empty table, placed their totes on the floor, and settled into the white wicker lounge chairs. A waitress approached their table and set their drinks down.

"Ah, this is nice," Rosetta said, sipping her glass of raspberry Margarita.

"Yes, makes you almost forget about our room," Joyce said, sipping her glass of lemonade.

"Speaking of room, I pulled this off the nightstand under my reader," Rosetta said, reaching into her skirt pocket.

"The officer said not to touch anything."

"Yes, but I didn't want to risk the chance he or his assistant would take it, especially if it is from that young man from the airport," Rosetta said, setting her drink down on the table.

She opened the folded white sheet and read the words written inside.

"Hmm, what do you make of this?" she asked Joyce, handing the paper over to her.

"It says, 'Give it back.' What does that mean?" Joyce asked as she handed the sheet of paper back to Rosetta's outstretched hand.

Rosetta returned the paper sheet to her pocket and drank a few more gulps of her Margarita. Holding up her pointer finger for a second, she fished around in her tote bag and pulled the little book out just enough for her daughter to see it.

"Maybe it's this?" she said and returned it to her cloth bag.

"First someone gives it to you, and then someone wants it back. Sounds odd," Joyce said, taking another drink.

"Same person or not?" Rosetta murmured.

"Well, we can turn it in at the front desk. In the meantime, I'm getting hungry. Let's see if lunch is ready," Joyce said, rising from her chair

"Good idea. But I'm bothered why there are such cloak and dagger with these notes and the book?" Rosetta asked as she finished the last of her drink.

Gathering her tote bag, she followed Joyce through the lounge. Once they walked down the stairs, Rosetta said, "I'm going to hold onto this book a little while longer."

"Why?"

"To see if I can read it," Rosetta said as they entered the dining room. Joyce spotted an empty table.

"While you're doing that, I'm going to look over our map where we'll make stops along the river."

Chapter 12 – The Mystery

After their lunch, which had as much food as served at dinnertime, Rosetta and Joyce returned to their cabin to check if their room had been restored. Unlocking the door with her key card, Rosetta stepped inside. Everything looked in order. Before Joyce had a chance to close the door behind them, they heard someone rap on their door.

A woman in a staff uniform stood outside.

"Is everything all right now?" she asked in a thick German accent.

"Yes, everything looks good. Thank you," Rosetta replied. "Wait one minute."

Rosetta turned and withdrew two Euros from her pocket and gave them to the woman.

"Thank you, madam," she said and walked away.

Joyce set her tote on the floor beside their made beds. When Rosetta sat on the edge of hers, she pulled out the little book.

"Did you want to drop that off at the front desk now?" Joyce asked.

"No, I think I'll see if I can read this." Rosetta tried to read the words and shook her head. "It's some kind of Germanic language. I'm afraid it's too thick for me."

"Why don't you take photos of it with your cell phone? Then we can turn the book in and you still have a copy to translate. For now, I'm going to take a shower," Joyce announced.

Rosetta removed her waistcoat and hung it into the small closet. Walking over to the small desk near the balcony window, she sat down and began taking pictures with her cell phone. Once finished, she stood to retrieve her small camera from her bed and took the same page pictures just in case one of her devices got lost.

Through the thin wall, Joyce's shower rumbled as Rosetta continued to photograph the diary's entries. Setting her camera on the nightstand between the beds, she sat on the edge of her mattress and entered a phrase from the diary on her translation phone app. She continued this process until Joyce stepped out of the bathroom.

"Oh, that feels great," Joyce said, stepping out of the bathroom. She wiped her wet hair with one of the large towels.

"Good, I'm ready. I got everything photographed," Rosetta said, putting her camera back into her tote bag. "I'll take my shower now."

Afterward, Rosetta suggested she and her daughter sit on the roof deck.

"I'll return that book when we go to dinner," Rosetta said. "What I can't read, I'll try to translate more with my phone's translator app later."

"Can you read some of the German?" Joyce asked.

"Only a little bit. In my line of work, I encounter several people from Germany traveling into the capital. I'm ready if you are."

"Yes, I'm ready," Joyce replied."

Feeling refreshed from their showers, they picked up their steps and paused at the reception desk. Rosetta approached the steward behind the counter.

"Yes, ladies, how can I help you?" he asked.

"Someone dropped this when I attended the Melk Abbey tour there this morning. Would you please see that it's returned?" she asked the tall slender man.

The staff member nodded and smiled. He retrieved the little book from Rosetta's outstretched hand.

"Most happy to, madam. I had just received a call from the abbey. They wanted to know if the diary had been turned in. Thank you," he said.

"You're welcome. Come, Joyce, there's the stairway to the top deck. Let's see what's up there."

Joyce glanced back at the reception desk. She noted the steward attempted to insert the book into a drawer behind the counter. Turning her attention back to climbing the stairway, she followed her mother upstairs to the top deck.

Rosetta noticed several white-winged insects lying dead on the false green turf covering the center of the deck.

"Oh, dear, the fairies have died," Rosetta said, pointing at the tiny white moths.

"That's funny, Mom, not for the bugs though," Joyce said, smiling as the warm breeze brushed her cheeks.

They found an umbrella table to sit around where they could watch the bank of the river pass by their boat. Swans appeared and Joyce hurried over to the railing to take a few pictures.

"What's that boxy room over there?" Joyce asked, pointing to a structure on the boat a third of the way from the bow.

"That is the wheelhouse, where the captain steers the boat," Rosetta said. "The cabin rises above the deck on hydraulics. When the riverboat moves into a water lock, the wheelhouse lowers down below the deck."

"How do you know that?" Joyce asked.

"I read about this boat before our trip. Lots of interesting information in the brochure," she said, opening her cell phone to her photos.

Rosetta looked at one of the book photos she took and entered the words into her translator. Then she wrote the translations down in her medium sized notebook.

"Listen to this. *'My love awaits me after dark. I will meet him in the woods just beyond the bridge.'*"

"That's beautiful, Mom. Must be a diary. How old do you think it is?" Joyce asked.

"There's a date on the first page but it's smudged. Fifteen, ah, I can't make out the rest."

Just as their boat was about to enter the first of sixty-four water locks, Joyce spotted an unusual sight on the grassy bank near the shore.

"Mom, come look! There are Canadian geese sitting there," she said, encouraging her mother to look.

"Are you sure?" Rosetta asked.

"Yes, come and look. There are lots of them."

Rosetta set her notebook down, pocketed her cell phone, and rose from her chair. Their boat inched closer to the enormous doors of the lock.

"Listen to this. *'My love awaits me after dark. I will meet him in the woods just beyond the bridge.'*"

"That's beautiful, Mom. Must be a diary. How old do you think it is?" Joyce asked.

"There's a date on the first page but it's smudged. Fifteen, ah, I can't make out the rest."

Just as their boat was about to enter the first of sixty-four water locks, Joyce spotted an unusual sight on the grassy bank near the shore.

"Mom, come look! There are Canadian geese sitting there," she said, encouraging her mother to look.

"Are you sure?" Rosetta asked.

"Yes, come and look. There are lots of them."

Rosetta set her notebook down, pocketed her cell phone, and stood up. Their boat inched closer to the enormous doors of the lock.

"Yes, I see them. I guess they migrate here too."

"Someone left a water bottle on the bow," Joyce remarked.

A uniformed man approached them.

"I heard you, miss. We use a water bottle as a height indicator that the boat would clear. If the water bottle tipped over by an overhead ridge of the lock, we would know the water level is too high. The captain would signal the lock operator to adjust the water capacity of the lock before our boat could float through the canal.

"I'm afraid you must go below. We will be lowering the helm in a few minutes," he said. "We have to have this deck cleared."

"Thank you. Oh, I almost forgot my notebook," Rosetta said, returning to their table.

Before they walked down the stairs, they saw crewmen disassembling tables, umbrellas, and folding the patio chairs to lay flat on the deck.

A. Nation

As Rosetta and her daughter walked down the stairs, they watched from the open railing the rising cement wall surrounding their boat.

"Ugh, can you smell that pungent odor?" Joyce asked, wrinkling her nose in disgust.

"Wet moss," Rosetta replied.

As their boat dropped deeper into the locks, the internal rooms grew darker. The auto ceiling lights turned on when the sunlight faded.

"Let's go to the lounge. I think the program director is giving a talk," Rosetta said.

"Good idea. I could use a lemonade," Joyce replied.

They walked upstairs to the lounge. Rosetta heard many passengers near them express how claustrophobic they felt as their boat floated in the huge locking system. She and Joyce joined several other people to watch their boat float through the open gates.

"Hello, everyone. I am Hans Becker, your Program Director. If you notice this lock on this part of the river widens enough to accommodate two riverboats. Other locks up ahead may narrow, and allow only one boat at a time through," he said over the loudspeaker.

When they arrived at the lounge, Rosetta noticed their boat had lowered several feet as it glided ahead toward the lock gates. The boat floated within two inches next to the side of the cement wall.

"I feel like we are on a toy boat in a huge bathtub," Rosetta said.

"You look apprehensive, Mom. I'll order the drinks," Joyce said.

"Thank you, I am a little."

Joyce ordered their lemonades from the bartender while Rosetta located seats for them to enjoy the sunlight shafting over the cement walls. As their boat escaped to the other side of the locks, sighs of relief whispered from many of the passengers.

When Joyce returned, Rosetta accepted her cold drink. As the riverboat sailed under a large bridge, Rosetta frowned when she saw the graffiti on the cement footing.

"Will you look at that," Rosetta said, gesturing at the artwork.

"You would think Germany with their restrictive laws would prevent that," Joyce said as she sipped her lemonade through a straw.

"I guess they can't control everything. Look at the bleached water line. The river is down quite a bit," Rosetta observed as she stripped her straw from its paper wrapper.

"I'm not surprised in this heat," Joyce said, leaning back.

Then the Program Director spoke into the microphone for all to hear. "In the last few days, the water level has dropped due to the heat. At this time, we aren't worried about clearance at this location. However, we may have to switch boats coming from the north and bus you over to them."

"How will our bags get to the other boat?" someone asked.

"You need to have them packed and set out in the hallway the night before. I will keep you informed if that is the case," the director said. "The other boat is identical to this one, and you will have the same cabin numbers and views. Those of you who have scheduled a tour in the morning will do that as planned, but your driver will return you to the other boat on the Rhine River. That is all."

120

"Just another tour," Rosetta said and drank the last of her lemonade before rising.

"Maybe so, but I'm getting tired of packing and unpacking," Joyce said. "I'm going to get a cup of coffee to take back to our room. Do you want one?"

"I'll have a hot chocolate if there is one in that machine."

"Yes, there is. And cookies," Joyce replied, smiling.

Taking their drinks and treats with them, Rosetta and Joyce walked down the stairs to the main reception area. They strolled through the hallway until they arrived at their cabin door. Rosetta handed her cup and cookie to Joyce so she could insert her key card. Once it opened, she took her hot chocolate out of Joyce's hand to step inside of their cabin.

Joyce, passing her mother, placed their cookies on the counter near the water tray holding a carafe of water. She set her cup down on the counter in front of their beds. After pulling the drapery aside, she unlocked the glass balcony door, sliding it to one side. Sticking her head out toward the balcony, Joyce watched their boat drift past the cement wall of the receding water lock.

Rosetta set her hot cocoa cup near Joyce's cookies. She noticed her tote bag on her bed and decided to put it into the narrow closet, placing it on the floor. When she heard a tinny clink from her bag, she fished around the inside bottom. At first, she didn't find anything that would create that sound. Then she remembered placing some coins into the side pocket. Reaching inside, she found the coins. To her surprise, she also discovered an old rusty key.

"What is it, Mom?" Joyce asked when she saw her mother searching the tote.

"I just found this key. I don't know where it came from. It's not mine," Rosetta said, holding the piece of iron in the air.

"Maybe that young man in the airport placed it there," Joyce said, holding her drink and reaching for her cookie.

"No, I remember. Someone was in that old church where I fell asleep.

"You also fell asleep in the museum," Joyce said, smirking.

"Yes smarty, but in the church, I dreamt I saw a hand pass my side vision where I was sitting. When I woke up, there was no one in the church but me. Remember at the airport I only found that sheet of paper with Melk Abbey written on it."

"How strange. Why would anyone give you a key?" she asked, with one foot on the balcony floor and the other still in their room.

Rosetta opened her cell phone to look at the picture she had taken of the diary's cover.

"Well, I can tell it's not for the diary. The keyhole in my photo is shaped different."

"Maybe somebody is trying to tell you something. First, you received a note, then the diary, and now this key. Let's sit out here and talk about this some more."

Rosetta slipped her notebook and the key from her tote into the drawer of the nightstand. Picking up her insulated cocoa cup and her cookie, she took the far chair to her right in the narrow balcony. Placing her cup and the treat on the small plastic table between the two patio chairs, Rosetta sat down. Joyce, already seated, proceeded to sip from the plastic edge of her hot coffee cup. Together they watched the riverboat leave the water lock and sail past the cement embankment. Rosetta breathed in the fresh air and sighed.

"You don't think the key fits the diary?" Joyce asked.

"It's too big. Probably for a door lock," Rosetta surmised as she picked up her cup.

"Well, we don't have enough information. Let's just relax for now."

"I'm with you," Rosetta said, turning her thoughts away from the old key. She sipped more of her hot chocolate. "Oh, I wish your brother was here to enjoy this," she remarked.

"Yes, but we wouldn't see much of him while he's with his family. Give him a few years when his kids are grown," Joyce reminded her.

"I"ll be in a wheelchair by that time," Rosetta moaned.

"This has been a great trip, Mom, aside from the room mess, I still can't believe I'm in Europe. I feel I need to keep pinching myself to make sure this isn't a dream. And, I'm keeping lots of history notes for my thesis."

Rosetta smiled at her happy child as if she were looking at Joyce when she was eight years old. Then she turned her attention toward the ducks floating by the bank of the river. Finishing her hot chocolate and cookie, she rose and reentered their room.

She set the cup on the silver tray and sat on the edge of her bed. Pulling out her notebook from the nightstand drawer, she opened her cell phone to translate more of the diary's writings. *"This is beginning to sound like the story I've been reading,"* she thought as she jotted down a few translated words.

Then there was a knock on their cabin door.

Mystery Along the Danube

Chapter 13 - Investigation

Rosetta rose to answer their door. The security officer, who they had met earlier, stood in the hallway with another uniformed man. The other man wore a dark navy colored jacket as compared to the khaki one the rest of the riverboat crew wore.

"Yes?" Rosetta asked, opening the cabin door.

"This man is from the Austrian police. He would like to ask you more about the book you found," the boat security officer said.

"Of course, would you like to come in?" she asked.

Then she hesitated, realizing it how crowded it may be in their cabin. The security officer noticed her pause and offered her a better solution.

"Would you like to join us in better accommodations? We can talk on the top deck. You too, madam," he said, tilting his head as he motioned toward Joyce.

"Sure. Come on, Joyce," Rosetta said, following the security officer into the hallway.

Joyce closed their door and stepped behind Rosetta. The Austrian police officer took up the rear. They paced through the hallway and turned right at the reception desk. After they climbed the stairs to the top deck of the riverboat, the security officer gestured toward an empty table away from the few people under the center row of tables covered with umbrellas. The overcast sky hinted of rain but that only added to the humidity in the air. The ship's security officer allowed the women to sit first.

The police officer spoke in German. The boat's security officer nodded and turned to Rosetta.

"This officer is here because you are one of many who attended the tour to the Melk Abbey. We have interviewed others who were in your tour. Did you see anything out of the ordinary?" he asked.

Rosetta, surprised by the question, expected him to ask about the vintage book.

"Well, I—I'm ashamed to say because it was so hot and I was so tired, I fell asleep in a chair," she replied. "I dreamt about something I read in my book. When I heard voices, I didn't wake up right away until my daughter returned to get me to the tour bus on time."

"These voices, do you remember what they said?" the security officer translated from the police officer.

"I thought it was part of my dream or actors playing out a scene. You see, I have been reading a historical novel about this area and the abbey. I thought the dream was from my book. What's this all about?"

"One of the museum guards had been killed. We want to know what you saw."

"What? That's terrible. I had no idea. I am so sorry, but I really can't help you. I didn't open my eyes until my daughter called me to hurry. Oh, and then there was that little book," Rosetta muttered.

Joyce placed her hand on her mother's arm. Rosetta calmed down from the gesture.

After the officer translated to the officer, they both turned to look at Rosetta in surprise.

"What little book?" the boat's officer asked.

"When I woke up, a diary of some kind laid at my feet. It was old with handwriting I couldn't read. The language of the writing appeared to be in German but then I didn't know. I—"

"Mom, you turned that in at the Reservation Desk, Remember?" Joyce interjected.

Rosetta turned back to the officer.

"Yes, I turned it over to someone on staff. I'm sorry but I really didn't see anything else that could help you."

"And you madam?" he turned to ask Joyce, "Did you witness or hear anything?"

"No, I returned from the gift shop to find my mother. When I did, she was dozing in the chair like she said. I tapped her shoulder and after she woke up, we hurried back to the gift shop and out to our tour bus," Joyce relayed.

"I see," he said, writing in his notebook.

The two officers conversed for a few minutes in the German language. The security officer looked up as he turned toward Rosetta.

"Thank you, madam, you have been most helpful. You may leave but we may have further questions for you in the future," the security officer said.

"Can we leave the boat tomorrow for our tour?" Joyce asked.

"Yes," he replied.

Rosetta and Joyce rose from their chairs. They bid the officers goodbye and headed down the stairs to return to their cabin. Standing on the top step, Joyce noticed the two men remained in deep conversation in a language she didn't understand.

"Why did you interrupt me back there?" Rosetta asked Joyce after they entered their room.

Joyce closed the door.

"Something smells fishy," she said.

"I don't smell anything."

"No, I mean, those men got really interested in that book when you mentioned it. If someone on staff here is in on this death, we don't want the wrong people bothering us. I'm sure the officers are okay but I didn't want you to tell them you took pictures of the pages. There were passengers and a couple of stewards nearby that could've heard us. What about that key someone gave you at the church?" Joyce asked.

"Well, I certainly wasn't going to tell them about my photos. I guess I better put my camera and the key in the safe too," Rosetta said. "I honestly didn't hear anyone in that church."

"I believe you. Something tells me we better be careful who we discuss this with."

"Hmm, I sure didn't expect this kind of problem on this trip," Rosetta mumbled.

"I'll hit the shower first," Joyce said.

After they showered, they dressed in their finer clothes for dinner. Rosetta placed her notebook, their passports, her camera, and the mysterious rusty key into the room safe before setting the lock.

"I'm using our birth years as the code. Mine is first," Rosetta explained.

"Should be safe enough. Let's go," Joyce approved. Following her mother out of their cabin, they headed for the dining room.

"What do you mean all you have is the book? Where's the key?" Alfredo yelled through his cell phone.

"It was a miracle the woman even turned the book in. Good thing I pocketed it before my boss saw me. I'll get that to you tomorrow when we tour Passau," said the voice over the phone.

"But the key," Alfredo asked again.

"She didn't have the key when I searched her room. If she had it with her, that would explain it."

"I'll have one of my men meet you at the beer fest by the shore." Then he disconnected his call. "Mario," he shouted into his intercom system.

"Yeah, boss?" a man asked, poking his head passed the office door.

"Meet Geoff at the beer fest tomorrow."

"Right, boss," his assistant replied and shut the door.

Chapter 14 - Passau

Rosetta and Joyce sat down for breakfast and watched as their riverboat pulled in alongside another riverboat docked near the shore of Passau, Germany. Men from the crew tied the craft up to the adjoining boat.

They finished their breakfast and returned to their cabin to change into their walking attire. They looped the guide receiver cords around their necks. Joyce reached over the counter to pick up the day's newsletter.

"Says here in the boat's newsletter it's named Passau or the "City of Three Rivers" since it divides the Danube, the Inn, and the Ilz Rivers," Joyce read.

"And here I always thought there were just two rivers," Rosetta said.

"Most people think that's true," Joyce said and continued reading. "The Celtic tribes first settled along the rivers and later the land became part of the Holy Roman Empire in the seven hundreds."

"I didn't know that," Rosetta said as she gathered their totes from the small closet.

"And it was well known as a trade center for salt mining near Salzburg."

Handing over Joyce's tote, she added, "I suppose that's where the word 'salt' came from."

"Good guess. Later Passau became known for their high-quality knives and swords," Joyce added. "Maybe you should buy a knife?"

"With my luck, I'll stab myself. Well, I'm ready, let's go," Rosetta said, slinging her tote bag over her shoulders.

They walked out into the hallway, stopping first at the reception desk to pick up their bus tour cards. Joining several other passengers, they climbed up the stairs to cross over the top decks of both riverboats. Adjustments made by the crew allowed for the low elevation in the river. Using this side-by-side arrangement, the passengers could exit to shore in an easier fashion.

Rosetta spotted their tour guide and hurried to tap the electronic paddle. Once done, she could hear the guide speak through her earbuds.

"Local smiths stamped the high-quality sword blades with the likeness of the Passau wolf. Those who believed the superstitions thought the wolf emblem gave the warrior protection from his enemies.

"When fires spread across Passau in the seventeenth century, the town rebuilt itself in the baroque manner that you will see today. Many churches and patrician houses crowd around the Inn and the Danube Rivers. The fires didn't burn much of St. Stephen's Cathedral. An architect, Carlo Lurago, rebuilt many buildings with stucco and fresco works of art. The church, which I will point out to you, now holds the largest cathedral organ in the world. The church is at the end of our walking tour, so you may visit and listen to the organ if you wish.

"As you have noticed, there is a beer fest going on shore. If you have time after your tour, please visit the vendors for your souvenirs.

"Come on, everyone. Let's get on our bus and we will explore where the Holy Roman Empire's influence touched the town of Passau."

Rosetta and her daughter boarded their bus and found two seats to sit together. Once the bus began moving, their guide told a little more history of Passau.

"Many of you may believe the Holy Roman Empire was centered in Rome. This was not the case in 800 A.D. In the Kingdom of Germany, the Pope crowned Charlemagne as the first Holy Roman Emperor. This religious gesture brought together many of the smaller territories in Europe.

"Then in the thirteenth century, the Hapsburg Monarchy expanded their territories outside the Roman Empire. The Hapsburgs functioned as a separate entity, but remain in the Pope's favor," their guide finished and sat down.

Joyce turned to Rosetta to ask, "Granola bar?" She held out the nut treat she had stored in her tote bag.

Rosetta giggled.

"No thanks, I ate more than I should at breakfast," she said, folding her hands across her lap.

Joyce returned the extra bar to her tote bag. She peeled the paper away from hers and took a bite from the nut and caramel confection.

The bus drove on through the city and passed several buildings with white gothic statues perched above them on the roof corners. Crossing a large square of asphalt and cobblestones, the bus came to a halt.

"Everyone, we will step out here and walk into the royal palace," their guide announced.

The tour group followed their guide up the front stairs to a large wooden double door latticed with iron hinges and metalwork. Their guide led them through the hallway and

A. Nation

into a room decorated with painted walls and frescoed reliefs.

Many members of the group made a restroom break and after ten minutes, the tour continued. Rosetta walked over to stand near Joyce.

"Who are you texting?" Rosetta asked, frowning since they came all this way to learn the culture of the country.

"Not texting. I'm writing myself notes so I can rewrite about this building later."

Her daughter laughed and followed behind her. As the guide moved on, Rosetta followed behind a couple in the tour group. Then the tour guide stopped and indicated for everyone to follow her into the next room.

"Isn't this room beautiful?" she asked Joyce.

At first, when she didn't receive an answer, she assumed Joyce was typing in more information on her cell phone. Rosetta looked around for her daughter.

"Joyce?" she asked.

When Joyce didn't appear, Rosetta called louder. The guide walked over to her.

"Is there a problem?" she asked.

"Yes, my daughter is gone."

"Maybe she's in the restroom?"

"Please wait, I'll check," Rosetta said and rushed to the restroom where they had been.

Looking down the intersecting hallway and in the restroom, she called Joyce's name several times. After a search, she yielded no results. Her heart beat faster in a rising panic. *"Where could have she gone?"* she asked herself.

Stepping out of the restroom, the guide approached her.

"Is she there?"

"No, she was right behind me before we entered this room," Rosetta wailed.

"Please sit down here," the guide said, gesturing to the wall bench. "I will contact security," the guide said.

"I'm not leaving until I find Joyce," Rosetta said, folding her hands on her lap and gazing around at the tour group.

She pulled out her cell phone and turned off the airplane mode. She and Joyce both agreed, while on the boat, they would turn their phones to airplane mode and use the ship's Wi-Fi. If they separated for some reason, they would turn the airplane mode off.

Dialing her daughter's phone, she heard the ringing but no one answered. Hesitating, at first, to put her phone away, she slipped it back into her pants pocket. After ten minutes, she watched as a security guard meet with her guide. The officer walked over to Rosetta.

"Madam, what does your daughter look like?" he asked.

"Oh, uh, short blond hair, she's thin and twenty years old. Here, I'll show you her photo," she said, retrieving her cell phone again. Scrolling down through the photos she had taken yesterday, she showed the guard a picture of her daughter standing by the stature of President Reagan. "Oh, I can't imagine where she is. Please help me," Rosetta cried on the verge of tears.

"Please calm down, madam. I'll have a look around and locate your daughter," he said.

Rosetta's frightened mind imagined all types of scenarios. *"Did she fall? Did she walk back to another room? Maybe she forgot something on the bus and went back to look,"* Rosetta fretted to herself. When the security guard returned without Joyce, she panicked.

"My daughter, what are you going to do?" she asked the man from security. Her heart raced and pounded against her ribs.

"I have sent several officers to look for her."

Rosetta's cell phone began ringing.

Grabbing the device out of her pocket, she pressed the green icon and answered.

"Hello, hello, Joyce?" she said, choking on her words.

Instead of Joyce, a deep male voice came on the line.

"Do you have the key?" he said.

Rosetta was so shocked, she didn't know how to answer.

"Is that your daughter?" the tour guide inquired.

Rosetta shook her head.

"Where's my daughter?" Rosetta managed to ask.

"Do you have the key or not?" the man on the phone growled.

"Uh, it's not with me right now. Can I speak to Joyce?"

She heard a short scuffle in the background and a woman's voice yelled, "Mom!"

"Joyce?"

From the corner of her eye, she could see the guide relaying information to the security guard.

"I will get you the key. But I have to return to my boat to get it," she sputtered to the caller.

"I will call you back. You have one hour or you won't see your daughter again," the caller growled and hung up.

For a second, she stared at her disconnected cell phone. Stunned, she turned toward the waiting tour guide.

"I have to get back to the boat. This man has my daughter and he's giving me one hour to wait for his call," she blurted out.

The guide and the officer conversed for a few minutes. The guide looked up as she turned toward Rosetta.

"I have instructed him to keep looking for your daughter after we leave the museum. Come with me and we will get you back onboard. What did the caller want?" she asked.

"Uh, money. Let's go," Rosetta replied, trying to avoid specifics.

"Do you have a lot of money on board the boat?"

"Some, but if I don't do what the man says, no telling what he would do to my daughter."

"All right. Return to the bus and I'll let the officers here know what is going on," the guide said.

Rosetta didn't want word of what the man on the telephone said to spread to anyone. Her chest was pounding. *"I need time to think first,"* she thought. Once she climbed into the bus and sat down next to the window, she began to shake. A male passenger across the aisle bent over toward her. She had seen the older man before in the boat's dining room.

"Ma'am, are you all right?" he asked, expressing concern.

"No, no, my daughter is missing," Rosetta bawled.

The man moved over to sit in the empty seat beside her.

"I'm sure she'll be found safe and sound," he assured her with a pat on her shoulder.

He handed her his handkerchief from his chest pocket. Rosetta accepted the white cloth and dried her swollen eyes.

"Thank you. I'm sorry if I'm a mess," she quivered.

"That's all right. Are the police looking for her?" he asked as she returned his handkerchief back to him.

"Yes, but when I left the palace, they hadn't found her. Oh, this is terrible. I think someone took my daughter. All over a stupid—oh, never mind."

"You mean she was kidnapped?" he asked.

Rosetta nodded. Thirty minutes now have passed. She could feel her anxiety raise her blood pressure.

"Is this your first trip to Europe?" the man asked, trying to distract Rosetta's mind away from her terrible ordeal.

She nodded and drew a tissue from her tote to wipe her nose. About that time, the tour guide came back to her seat. The older gentleman resumed his seat across the aisle. The guide sat down beside her.

"I have been in touch with security at the museum and they are reviewing the hallway cameras."

"Good. I just have to get back on board the boat in—," Rosetta said, looking at the time on her wristwatch. She gasped. "Oh God, in fifteen minutes! Can't the driver go any faster?"

"He's doing his best. I'm calling the boat to make sure you have first access to walk onboard," she said.

"Thank you. What will happen if my daughter doesn't come back before the boat sails?" Rosetta whined.

"As soon as we know where she is, we will send a cab to pick her up and meet us at one of the river ports up ahead."

The word of Rosetta's missing daughter spread like wildfire around the passengers on the bus. When the bus parked by their boat, all the passengers remained seated until Rosetta could leave the bus. Rosetta stood up and scrambled off the bus without any hindrance.

Merry participants from the beer festival spilled out onto the dock, impeding her way toward the boat. Rosetta thought she felt a tug on her tote strap, but when she turned around, everyone was drinking a glass of beer and smiling. Struggling through the jovial crowd of people, she ran to the gangway and hurried across the double decks of the two riverboats. Racing down the stairs, she almost tripped off the last step when a steward caught her under her arm just in time. Giving him a brief 'thank you,' she ran down the hallway to her cabin.

Her nervous fingers fumbled to pull her key card from her pants pocket. Unlocking her door, she stepped into her room. Making sure she latched her door, she entered the bathroom to splash water on her face. Leaving the restroom door ajar, she sat in the single chair in the room and tried to plan what to do next when the man called. Taking a slow deep breath, she calmed down. Walking over to the closet, she slid the door open, revealing the small safe on the shelf. Rosetta tapped the code on the keypad to unlock the safe. Opening the small safe door, she extended her hand in to retrieve the brown key lying inside.

Her phone rang. Startled, she pulled out her cell phone too fast from her pocket. It slipped out of her hand and fell to the floor. Wrapping her fingers around the device, she pressed the small green icon on the screen.

"Yes?" she asked, as her hands shook.

"Do you have the key?" the deep voice asked.

"Yes, yes. Is my daughter okay? Can I talk to her?" Rosetta blurted out.

"When you take your tour in Regensburg, I'll have someone meet you there."

"But I wasn't touring—" she tried to say, but the caller had hung up.

She jumped when someone knocked on her cabin door.

Closing the bathroom door that still stuck out in the room, she peered first through the peephole in the middle of the cabin door. Recognizing the Program Director, she opened the door a short ways.

"I heard about your daughter. I want to assure you this cruise line and every official on shore is searching for her. Is there anything I can do to help you with at this time, madam?" he asked, standing straight as a yardstick in his uniform.

"Uh, just I have to change my touring itinerary."

"I can help you with that. Do you wish to change it now?"

"No, I'll see you later. Thank you." She had to think. *"Can she trust the Program Director?"*

She paused and remembered her tour cards in her pocket.

"Wait, you can take these," she said, extending the cards toward him.

"Yes, madam. Thank you," he replied accepting the cards.

He smiled at her and walked down the hallway. Rosetta closed her door and slumped on the edge of her bed. Gazing over to where her daughter would sleep made her feel hollow inside. She moved over to Joyce's bed and laid down. She needed to think.

"Oh, dear Joyce, what have I gotten you into?" she murmured and cried herself to sleep.

When Rosetta woke up, the room had darkened. The sunlight she remembered from the afternoon no longer showed through the curtains. She looked at her watch and jumped off the bed. The time was 6:30 p.m. She wasn't real hungry, but she knew she had to keep up her strength. She decided to go to the Reservation desk to change her tour package and see what she could stomach from the buffet in the lounge.

"Yes, may I help you?" asked the young receptionist, standing behind the counter.

"Yes, I need to cancel my tour at the Bavarian Village Museum.

"Yes, but you know we can't refund the paid tours," The duty clerk said. The tours with these cruises are either inclusive or optional for purchase.

"I know. I want to take the Regensburg tour instead. Would that be all right?"

"Let me check," she said, leaning toward her computer screen. "We have two seats left on the bus. There is no charge. Will your daughter join you?"

"Good. No one told her." Rosetta took a deep breath. She didn't want to cry. "No, just me," she replied, refraining from spilling her guts to the young woman.

"All changed. Just pick up your travel card in the morning. The tour leaves at 8:45 a.m."

"Thank you," Rosetta said and left the reception desk to head up the stairs toward the lounge.

Trudging upstairs, she thought her shoes were filled with lead. Even after the nap, she had taken, Joyce's dilemma still weighed heavy on her mind. There were fewer people in the lounge at this hour due to dinner serving in the main dining room. Stepping outside onto the bow, she walked over to the buffet tables.

She chose a sample of spaghetti, bratwurst, and chocolate pudding. She knew she had to have the extra calories to be alert in case that despicable man called her again. So far no one asked her where Joyce was, which relieved her. She didn't feel like talking about the kidnapping. Taking her small portions back to the middle of the deck, she climbed the stairs to the top deck of the riverboat.

Locating an empty seat, she set her dish on the table. Just as she sat down, a waiter walked toward her.

"Would you like anything to drink from the bar, madam?" he asked, holding a tray of used glasses he had picked up.

Rosetta looked at her moderate caloric plate and back at the steward.

"Thank you, I'll have some lemonade, please," she said.

She pulled out the fork from the wrapped napkin she had collected from the buffet and pecked at the spaghetti. By the time, the waiter had returned with her drink, she had eaten half of the noodles from her plate.

Rosetta curled a few strands of the pasta around her fork and managed to eat that. Her tongue detected no flavor. Cutting one of the meatballs in fourths, she forced a section down. It too was tasteless to her palette. Putting her fork down on her plate, she brought her hands up to her face and pushed her cheeks back. Sipping a little of the lemonade, she stared at her dinner plate and decided she couldn't finish the rest of the food. Then a male voice spoke to her from behind her chair.

"Is this seat taken?" he asked.

She looked up and recognized the older man from the bus. He was taller than she thought when she first saw him, but he was sitting at the time.

"You should keep your strength up," he said and sat in the chair beside hers. Holding his drink, he set it on the table.

"I should, but my stomach says 'no.' Are you alone on this trip? I remembered you weren't sitting by anyone on the bus."

"I'm traveling with friends. My wife passed a few years ago. By the way, my name is Tom, I'm from Ohio," he relayed.

141

"Oh, I'm sorry. I'm Rosetta, from D.C., divorced," she said and poked the half meatball on her plate.

"Good to know you, Rosetta. You know, if you eat that meatball, I'll help you find your daughter," he kidded, crinkling his eyes. "Have you heard any more from the kidnappers?"

"Just when I got back to the boat, he called and told me someone will meet me in Regensburg."

She brought the portion of meatball to eat it, but when the smell reached her nostrils, she put the fork back down.

"I can't eat that. Maybe I'll try the pudding." Taking up her spoon, she dug into the chocolate custard. That she could tolerate.

"No matter, the pudding is fine. Why do you think someone would kidnap your daughter?" he asked.

"I have something they want. I had to change my plans and take the Regensburg tour walk tomorrow. Which tour are you going on?"

"I'm taking that one as well," he said, sipping his wine from his glass.

Rosetta didn't know how much to trust this man. So far he hadn't asked what the kidnappers want. She made her excuse to leave.

"You've been kind but I really need my rest. I'll see you tomorrow," she said. Taking one more gulp of her lemonade, she rose from her chair.

"Yes, tomorrow," he replied, raising his glass in a gestured toast. As she headed for the stairs, she noticed he remained seated as she stepped down onto the first step.

She passed the dining room and walked down the hallway. Rosetta keyed her door lock and entered her cabin. Removing her cardigan, she draped it next to Joyce's clothes in the closet. Feeling her daughter's blouse between her fingers caused a tear to flow down her cheek. After a quick wash in the restroom, Rosetta crawled into bed and wished this all was a bad dream.

Chapter 15 - Regensburg

The next morning, Rosetta looked out through the sliding glass door to the balcony. She turned and walked to the closet shelf where the safe held her valuables. Opening the safe, she placed the old key into her passport purse she wore under her blouse.

Walking down to the dining room, which was empty at this early hour, she noticed one couple at the end of the room. Locating another empty table, she waited until the waiter came by with the morning drinks.

"I'll just have orange juice and I'll serve myself from the buffet," she said.

He nodded. As soon as he walked away, she rose to see what she could eat. Deciding the scrambled eggs looked palatable, she picked up some wheat toast. Returning to her six-person table, she was relieved no one else sat down. Rosetta ate what she could, making a sandwich with her toast and eggs. When she finished eating, she took a few moments to transcribe a few more words from her phone's photo of the diary.

A few more passengers entered the dining room. Not wanting to hold a conversation, Rosetta stood and made her way back to the reception area to wait for her tour bus to arrive. She approached the desk clerk.

"Excuse me, have you heard of any more about my daughter, Joyce Blessing?" she asked.

"I'm sorry, madam. We have not," the young woman replied.

Downhearted, Rosetta sat on the vinyl bench.

When the program director announced the tour she would take, she followed the rest of the touring passengers out the door toward the gangway. She grabbed a bottle of water from a nearby table provided by the boat staff. Then she stopped to ask the steward, handing the bottles out a question.

"Tell me. If someone doesn't return your receivers," she began, pointing to the one around her neck, "Is there a way you can locate these if they get lost?"

"It depends how far away the device is. Most of the time, someone from shore drops them off here or at our travel stations in the towns we visit," the uniformed man said.

Nodding, Rosetta moved toward the gangway and walked with the other passengers on shore. She looked around for the tour guide. Locating his paddle with the number of the tour she was taking, she tapped it for activation. Someone touched her on the shoulder.

"Good to see you this morning," the familiar voice said.

"Oh, hi, Tom. You too," she said, turning around and forcing a smile.

The passengers connected their receivers to their guide's paddle and climbed into their tour bus. Tom followed Rosetta.

"Do you mind if I sit next to you?" he asked.

"No, it's fine."

"Hello, everyone," the guide's voice announced over the bus speakers.

"Hello," the passengers answered.

"Let me tell you a little bit about Regensburg," began their guide. "This is a Bavarian German city well known for its medieval style of architecture. In the sixth century, the ruling family of Agilolfings controlled the land. A famous pope came from here, Pope Benedict XVI. At the age of five years old, Joseph Ratzinger wanted to be a cardinal because he loved the colorful vestments. During the rise of Hitler, the German army forced him into the army and later after the allies freed the country, he spent time in a prisoner of war camp. He served the church in many capacities from cardinal to archbishop. In 2005, he became Pope and later retired in 2013.

"When we take our walk, I'll point out the many gothic styles of the buildings and end our walk at St. Peter's Cathedral."

"Sounds fascinating," Tom murmured.

"Yes, it does. I do hope we can find Joyce."

Joyce awoke. Her wrists hurt from the ropes, which tied her to a chair. *"How long have I been here?"* she asked herself. She remembered a long drive, blindfolded. She woke up lying down on the back seat of a car with her hands tied behind her back. Someone reached over and placed a damp cloth over her face that smelled. It was the last thing she remembered before now.

"Where am I? Why have you brought me here?" she asked.

The man said nothing as he escorted her down a hallway lined with paintings until he turned right. He opened a door and pushed her into a small room. She caught herself before she stumbled to the floor. The man slammed the wooden door when she glanced back at him. His footsteps faded away. Rubbing her freed wrists, she looked around at a metal framed bed, an old chest of drawers against the wall, and a small inset of a closet to her left. She started pacing back and forth across the tiled floor.

"Where am I?" she asked herself. Joyce rubbed her wrists where the rope ties cut off her circulation. Her anger rose as she realized these people are using her to get to her mother. *"Who are they?"*

The door clicked. Joyce froze and stared at the impenetrable door. She tensed by the sound of the door unlocking, but it opened just a couple of feet.

"Step back, I'm bringing you food," a female voice uttered as she appeared through the slight opening.

An older woman about her mother's age walked in with a tray of cups and bowls. Joyce noticed a man standing in the doorway barricading the egress. He wasn't the same man who kidnapped her or who brought her to this room. By his frowning expression, she knew he wouldn't let her pass, even if she tried.

"You must eat," the stocky woman said in a thick accent Joyce couldn't place. "You're too thin, eat."

Joyce had to admit to herself, the hunger in her stomach growled at her. She picked up the toast by the covered bowl and ate a couple of bites.

"Good," the woman said and turned to march out through the doorway.

The man held the door open for the woman as she left. Joyce picked up the lid from the warm bowl and realized it looked like the Hungarian Goulash she and her mother had on one of the tours. This bowl of red soup, however, had a layer of grease floating on top. She picked up the spoon and skimmed off the puddles of fat.

The large man still stood in the doorway. Satisfied she was eating, he pulled the door closed, leaving her alone again. Joyce couldn't help but turn her head toward the door when she heard the sharp click in the keyhole.

She gulped down several spoonfuls of meat and potatoes until the hunger pains eased away. Looking around the small austere room, she noticed a tiny aperture in the wall near the ceiling above the bed. Sunlight wavered through the opening, lighting up her quarters. A wooden chest of drawers stood at the foot of her single framed bed with a nightstand comprised of straight legs with no drawers. This basic structure reminded Joyce of Amish furniture.

A small metal cross was the only decoration on the wall lit by the shaft of sunlight. She guessed this room could've served a monk in his day of solitude. The wooden door her captor shut had metal hinges on one edge. In the upper center, she noticed a small barred square hatch. Joyce guessed her guard could speak to her through the gated panel.

Picking at her food, she ate most of the goulash and toast. Under another covered plate, she found more potatoes and bratwurst. Not finding the sausage appetizing she ate one of the small potatoes. She picked up a cup of black liquid, she guessed to be strong tea. The brew didn't taste anything like coffee.

Glancing up toward the small window above her, she wondered if she could see outside and call for help. Setting the tray on the nightstand, she stepped toward the chest of drawers near the foot of the metal bed.

Pushing the heavy wooden bureau was easier than she thought. But when it scraped the tiled floor, a sharp noise screeched rang out. That stopped her. When no one came to her door, Joyce pulled out the four drawers and laid them on the narrow bed. Lifting the dresser from the sides, she swung it facing the wall to her right. Disappointment rose when she discovered the corner of the bed needed to move a couple more inches.

Removing the drawers from the bed and laying them with care onto the floor, she tried lifting the iron-framed bed. When she managed to raise it, the frame slipped out of her weak hands and created a thump on the floor. She stopped and straightened up, hoping the noise wouldn't attract her jailers. She soon discovered her guard heard her when he opened the little panel in the door.

"What's going on in there," shouted a gruff German voice in English through the small barred opening.

"Nothing, I just tripped. Leave me alone. I want to sleep," she called back.

The guard growled something she didn't understand and slammed the tiny door window shut. Hurrying to the end of the bed, she managed to move it an inch away from the chest. The heavy wooden chest stood about five feet in height. Standing on the bed mattress, Joyce was able to lift herself to the top of the bureau. She steadied herself and rose to a standing position. She discovered the little vent didn't have any glass. When she peered over a series of rooftops, the sight dismayed her.

Below her, she saw an empty courtyard to the left surrounded by white stucco buildings. Beyond this structure were rolling green hills of vineyards. Nobody would hear her even if she yelled. Crouching, she sat down on top of the chest and stretched her legs to the mattress. Swinging the bureau back to its original position against the other wall, she began replacing the drawers. *"I'll have to figure out another way out of here,"* she told herself.

"I heard noise coming from that woman's room," Alfredo growled at his underling. "Are you sure she can't escape?"

"Yes, sir. When I looked in on her, she had moved the chest of drawers and the bed. But even if she could fit through the window, there's nowhere for her to go," his employee replied.

"Better not be. I just received word from my contact at the riverboat. He says the girl's mother is taking the Regensburg tour. Let's take a drive," Alfredo said, grabbing his khaki fedora hat.

"Yes, sir. I have the car waiting for you."

Rosetta watched the bicyclists through the side window of the bus traveling along on the pathways near the highway.

"I love the way these European cities have rebuilt their buildings back into the style they once were before the war," Tom observed.

"Yes, they are lovely," she sighed.

Her heart just wasn't in the mood for sightseeing.

"Then we gave these countries lots of money to rebuild after the war," Tom added.

"Huh? Oh, I'm sorry. I just can't concentrate."

Tom reached over and tapped the top of her left hand.

"Try not to worry. We will find her. Don't give up hope," he assured her.

"Thank you. But what if they don't bring Joyce to Regensburg?"

Their bus slowed.

"It looks like we're stopping. I'm turning on my receiver," she said.

After their bus parked, their guide stood up and explained where they would take their walking tour.

"First, we will cross the square to the municipal building over there," he pointed, "The archway is where we will enter. Once we have finished the tour, I want all of you to meet me at the fountain in the center of this square. Can everyone see the statue in the center of the fountain?

Many of the passengers replied, "Yes."

"Good. Let us proceed," he said and began walking.

Rosetta and Tom followed their guide over to the fountain before starting their tour. Rising from the falling waters was a statue of a man on a horse surrounded by alabaster angels with their faces frozen in time. As soon as their guide motioned for everyone to proceed, he began relating the history.

Chapter 16 — Tap-Tap-Tap

Joyce heard a key turn in the keyhole of her cell door. The same stout woman entered, holding a meal tray with her food. A different man from the others she had seen stood near the doorframe. He waited until the woman left before he entered and closed the door behind him. He had a broad square body with thick hands. His scarred face looked at her.

She grabbed a spoon from the food tray. Her nerves rose in anticipation. *"What does this man want?"* she asked, fearing the worse.

"You can put that down. I'm only here to talk to you," he said in a deep voice.

"Who are you and why am I here?" she asked.

Joyce's fingers held onto the utensil as tight as she could. She wasn't taking any chances with this man.

"I am Alfredo. Here, you may have your passport back. I was under the mistaken impression you were Gloria Montaign. Are you familiar with her?"

"No, I never heard of the woman. Can I leave now?" Joyce asked.

"In time. We are waiting for your partner."

"Partner?" Joyce asked, peering up at his fat jowls.

"Yes, the woman traveling with you who is using my friend's travel ticket."

Joyce looked him in the eye.

"Your friend is dead. Don't you read the newspapers? My mother works at the travel agency where she got the tickets. Her boss said she could use them."

"I see, but she has the key, does she not?"

"We have lots of keys. Which one are you referring to?" Joyce asked, not prepared for his next reaction.

The man swung his arm high and slapped her across the face, leaving a red welt on her cheek.

"I will not tolerate insolence," he growled.

The force from his slap loosened her grip on the teaspoon, as it went flying across the bed. Joyce, knocked off balance, slid off the bed's edge before she hit the floor. Rubbing her face with the back of her hand, she looked up at him. Her anger rose more than her fear.

Gathering his composure, his puffy face bent down toward her. Joyce leaned back, holding her hands up in case he tried to hit her again.

"As soon as your mother arrives with the key, we will transport you to the nearest consulate," he said, turning toward the closed door.

Looking back at her, he added, "and don't waste your time trying to escape. You won't."

He jerked the door open, shutting it with a slam after he left the small room. The scrape of his key turned in the door lock.

She wanted to cry but the tears wouldn't come. Her arms gripped tight around the limp pillow as she thought about the man and her situation. *"How dare he treat me this way? I'm an American citizen. He'll regret treating me this way after I get out of here,"* she told herself. Lying down on the lumpy mattress, Joyce stared at the patterned ceiling.

Gazing at the stucco plaster on the ceiling, she formed impressions from the swirling design of imagined faces looking down on her. She rolled over on her side and tried to close her eyes, but sleep wouldn't come. As she opened an eye, she stared at the narrow closet across the room recessed in the wall. She sat up, realizing this may be her way out.

Rising off the bed, she stepped toward the closet. The open two-foot wide space held a wooden bar crossing the archway to hang clothes, but she didn't see any hangers. Joyce looked inside and peered upward into the darkened cavity. She thought she saw a dark-colored square in the ceiling.

"Sometimes," she muttered, "these old places have to have access for electricals or plumbing."

Without hesitation, she pocketed the spoon and pulled off the bedsheet. She stuffed the corners of the sheet under each of the bed's metal feet.

This time, pulling on the bed frame, she slid the bed over the tiled floor toward the closet without a sound. Joyce found the narrow end of the bed wouldn't fit inside the archway until she removed the mattress, and shoved the cot end first into the closet. She laid the single pillow on top of the bare metallic springs and removed her shoes before climbing on the bed frame to stand on a softer surface. Then she pulled off her socks and stuffed them into her pants pocket.

Reaching upward, she placed the flat of her hand on the panel in the ceiling. Touching the cold metal sheet above her head, she bent her elbows outward and shoved the

154

cover to one side. Feeling around inside, she felt a hard beam of wood edged along the opening. "This is just like rock climbing," she thought as she reached into the cavity, locating a handhold.

Her fingers enveloped around the edge of the beam as she 'walked' her bare feet up the rough stucco wall in the closet. Lifting her torso over the edge of the ceiling opening, Joyce stretched her arm out and found a cold metal bar to grab. Pulling as hard as she could, she lifted her knee onto the beamed edge and disappeared into the dark shaft.

Hooking her toes on the edge of the metal panel, she managed to slide it back into place. Her hands felt dusty from centuries of grime as she crawled away from her prison cell. The tight crawl space forced her to twist and turn as she advanced past several rooms below. Some furry thing brushed against her bare foot. She slapped the back of her hand against her mouth to stop herself from screaming. In the distance, a small rodent squeaked and tapped its nails as it ran down through the shaft ahead of her.

Recovering her composure, she crawled on until her knee set down on something sharp. "Ow! What's this?" she whispered.

Rosetta's tour group meandered through the hallway of the Würzburg Residence, a former school building now used for government and business offices. Their guide continued his talk.

"Before the war, this was a residential school for young boys. If you noticed as you walked in, this building is U-shaped. One three-story arm housed the students and the other, where we will exit, accommodated the professors. The domed roof covered the classrooms and the library in the center of the structure. Follow me," he said, pushing in two large wooden doors. The tour group followed him and soon found themselves in a large amphitheater.

Rosetta hung back toward the entry, hoping someone would ask her for the old key. Tom stepped forward to take a photo with his camera. When the guide finished his dissertation, he led everyone back into the hallway. Rosetta waited until Tom walked by and joined him.

As they walked through the center of the building, the tour group noticed the large dome ceiling looming above them. Rosetta adjusted her earpiece to hear their guide speak through her receiver.

"During the war, the two residence halls were destroyed. Thanks to an American airman, the domed roof and our valuable paintings were preserved."

In deep thought about her daughter, Rosetta realized what the guide said and tapped Tom's shoulder.

"What was the airman's name," she asked.

"Sorry, I didn't catch it," Tom said and walked on with the group of people to the other side of the room.

Rosetta lagged behind and when she passed the curve of the wall, she thought she heard thumping behind her. Shrugging the sound off as construction work, she hurried to catch up with Tom and the group.

Just as she was about to leave the domed room, a familiar set of knocks sounded in the distance. The tapping sounded like Joyce's code. *"Joyce!"* she thought. She ran back to the entrance of the wide room and listened to the 'tap tap (pause) tap tap. *"Where is that coming from?"* she asked herself. Walking further, the tapping sound faded. Her frantic fingers tapped the wall in return, but she received no response. Rosetta stepped back and forth, tapping on the wallpaper until she heard a muffled rapping behind a hanging portrait.

Glancing in both directions, she didn't see anyone to stop her or ask to help her get the painting down. *"Where is security when you need them?"* Used to doing tasks by herself, she didn't want to risk leaving this spot.

She stretched her arms and reached up to lift the portrait off its clip, but the heavy frame came down too fast for her. Struggling to set it down against the wall, it slipped out of her hands, thumping hard on the floor. One corner scratched a spot of the wallpaper running along the lower portion of the baseboard.

Tapping once again on the upper stucco section, she thought she heard a response. Then a louder knock and another to her left came from the other side of the wall. When a third thump sounded behind a small wooden door, Rosetta rapped as loud as she could.

"Joyce, is that you?" she called.

Delighted when the tapping code resumed, she turned the paint peeled doorknob. It jammed at first but moved when she twisted it again. Glancing once down the hall, she still didn't see anyone. Jiggling the knob, Rosetta managed to open the door. Joyce burst out and wrapped her arms around Rosetta's shoulders.

"Joyce!" Rosetta exclaimed, returning an embrace.

Rosetta looked over her smudged daughter's face, her torn Capri at one knee, and her bare feet.

"Mom. Come on. Let's get out of here or they'll come looking for me," she said.

"Over my dead body. Where are your shoes? Never mind, you can tell me later. Let's get you out of here," Rosetta said, encircling her shoulders.

Joyce pulled her socks out of her pockets and covered her bare feet. They hurried down the hallway until Rosetta caught sight of the tour group entering the gift shop. When she spotted her guide and a security officer, she and Joyce approached them.

"Sorry if I'm holding you up, but I just found my daughter, Joyce Blessing. Someone had taken her from our last port stop."

"Are you all right?" their guide asked Joyce.

"Yes, I can tell you what I know," Joyce said.

Their guide directed her to the security officer standing in the hallway. After the guide explained to him what Joyce had been through, he took her aside while Rosetta and their guide waiting by the exit door. After ten minutes, Joyce joined them.

"Can I leave this with our guide?" Rosetta asked.

The officer nodded and walked through the exit doors with them. Slowing down their pace, they followed the touring patrons outside to meet with their guide by the center fountain in the open square.

Rosetta turned to Joyce who stood behind the fountain's shade. Joyce danced back and forth on the warm cobblestones.

"Ouch! Mom, these cobblestones are hot in the sun," Joyce yelped, dancing back and forth.

"Do you want to run for the bus? It's over there," Rosetta suggested.

"No, I'll wait in the shade. I don't want those nasty people to see us in the open," Joyce replied.

"Good idea. I can see our guide waving over there. Good thing you have socks on. Wait a minute. I threw my gloves into my tote this morning just in case my hands got cold in these drafty buildings. Here they are. Slip these on," Rosetta offered, pulling the large gloves out of her tote bag.

Joyce took them and stretched them over her toes, leaving the cloth fingers flopping.

"Thanks, better than nothing."

The tour group started strolling toward their bus. Tom caught up with Rosetta.

"You disappeared. Some of us were looking for you." He said.

"Sorry. Tom, this is my daughter, Joyce," Rosetta said as they waited their turn to enter the bus.

"What happened to you?" he asked Joyce, gazing at the dirt marks on her face and arms.

"I'd rather not talk about it now," Joyce said, stepping up the short stairway into the bus.

"We'll fill you in later, Tom," Rosetta added.

Joyce found a window seat and her mother joined her on the one near the aisle. Tom sat down near another man across the aisle from Rosetta. Joyce leaned over to whisper in her mother's ear.

"How friendly are you two?"

"Just acquaintances. You rest now. We'll buy you a pair of new shoes tomorrow.

Joyce laughed to assure her mother, "I have a pair of sneakers in my suitcase, but maybe some nice shoes would do."

The bus drive took less than thirty minutes to travel through the city and arrive back at their docked boat.

Hurrying down the gangway, they entered near the reception desk and dropped off their tour cards. Once they arrived at their cabin, Rosetta inserted her card key and allowed Joyce to enter first.

Joyce sat down on the edge of her bed. "I thought I'd never love this bed. But that contraption they had in that dingy room saved my life," she announced.

Rosetta watched her daughter pull off the gloves from her feet.

"I guess I owe you a pair of gloves. These look a bit roughed up," Joyce said, holding them up.

"Just throw them away. They were old anyway and I certainly don't need them in this European heat wave— drafty castle or not. So, what can you tell me? What happened to you?" Rosetta asked."

"So, what can you tell me? What happened to you?" Rosetta asked.

"I don't remember how they took me. I smelled something funny and the next thing I knew, I found myself tied up in a small bedroom. I found an escape through the ceiling using my rock climbing technique and crawled through the air vents until I came down into the room where you found me. I must have been tapping my knuckles out for over an hour, mainly to attract somebody. I'm glad it was you who heard me," she explained.

Joyce pulled out her suitcase from under her bed. Moving some of her clothes aside, she found her white tennis shoes.

"Wow, I'm proud of you. I'll never complain about your hobby again. I'm sure you'd want to shower. Why don't you go first," Rosetta said.

"Thanks, but before I do, have a look at this," Joyce said as she reached into her pants pocket. She stepped closer to her mother and held a strand of sparkling colors.

"What do you have there?" Rosetta asked, placing her hand under the string of jewels.

A. Nation

"A necklace, see the catch? I was crawling around in the air vent for a while and stumbled upon this lodged in the floor of the shaft. That's why the knee on my pants leg is torn. Good thing I have two more pairs of pants packed."

"Do you know what this is?" Rosetta asked, holding the jewels up.

"Someone's necklace?"

"Yes, a very old one," Rosetta said, admiring each jewel in their settings.

"Well, that man who held me said his name was Alfredo. I don't think he would've ever thought to find this in the ceiling. He wouldn't fit," Joyce laughed.

Rosetta set the strand down on the counter and rushed over to the nightstand. She opened her reader.

"You're going to read me a story?" Joyce asked, unsure why her mother picked up the device.

"No, I want to show you this picture. Centuries ago a beautiful necklace was stolen from a regional count. The red jewel in the center represented ownership and a treaty to his land holdings. When this necklace disappeared, the nearby viceroy claimed the property and the church proclaimed him and his new wife emperors. Joyce, look. It's the same necklace!" Rosetta exclaimed, pointing at the colored photo in her reader.

"But the center stone is missing. What are we going to do with it now?" Joyce asked, glancing at the picture and back at the glittering necklace.

"Well, I'm certainly not giving it to someone on this boat. I have to locate a policeman tomorrow and see what he says."

"I know, since they might not speak English, we can talk to our consulate in Cologne."

161

"Is there one there?" Rosetta asked.

"Yes, in my historical studies, we talked in class why it was built there after the war."

"That's the plan. First, we shower—then we go to dinner. And you, my lovely," Rosetta said to the necklace as she held it up. "I'll put you in our safe for now."

Rosetta rose off the edge of her bed and opened the closet door to the safe on the center shelf. Securing the safe, she closed the closet door. She watched Joyce walk into the restroom to moisten a washcloth. After her daughter washed her face, Rosetta picked up her hairbrush from the counter in front of the beds. Glancing over, she smiled as Joyce brushed her blond hair to one side of her face. Then she noticed a bruise on her daughter's forehead.

"Where did you get that mark on your face? In the vent crawling around?"

"No, Mr. Big hit me."

"Well, now I'm really mad," Rosetta said and reached over to hug her daughter. "I'm sorry I got you into this mess."

"It's all right, Mom. Uh, shower?"

"Yes, go ahead."

As Joyce entered the restroom and closed the door behind her, Rosetta wiped a tear from her cheeks. *Maybe we should just go home,"* she thought.

Chapter 17 – On Board

"She what!?" yelled Alfredo at his assistant.

"She escaped through the ceiling, boss," replied the man, shifting his feet.

"Get out of here!" Alfredo yelled once again.

Once his employee scurried out of his office, Alfredo made a phone call to his contact on the riverboat.

"The girl escaped. Have they returned to your boat? Good, now find that key," he demanded, punching his cell phone to disconnect the call. Gone were the good old days when you could slam a receiver down into the cradle for the satisfaction of hanging up. Frowning at the small device, he placed it into his jacket pocket and lifted his great girth out of his chair.

Clean once again, Rosetta and Joyce headed down the main deck for dinner in the dining room. As they passed the reception desk, one of the uniformed employees just hung up his cell phone. Strolling through the dining room, Rosetta spotted Tom sitting with another couple.

"May we sit with you?" Rosetta asked.

"Yes," Tom answered. "Oh, these are my friends, Barbara and Kevin."

"Are they your traveling friends?" Joyce asked.

"No, they are sitting at another table over there," he said, pointing passed the buffet counters.

When the couple at Tom's table, greeted them, Rosetta guessed from their accent, they were Australian. The thin woman smiled while her husband picked up his cloth napkin and laid it across his thigh.

"Good to meet you. I'm Rosetta and this is my daughter, Joyce."

Joyce returned a small smile and nodded.

"Were you the young lady missing from our tour group this afternoon?" Barbara asked.

"Yeah, I, uh, lost my way," Joyce said. She didn't desire any in-detailed discussion about her kidnapping.

The waiter arrived to take their drink orders. Relieved by the interruption, Joyce ordered a cola.

"But weren't you gone for two days?" the woman asked.

"I took a cab," Joyce replied and drank some of the water in a glass before her.

Changing the subject, Rosetta interjected, "Are you two going on the Nuremberg through History tour tomorrow?"

"No, we chose the Nuremberg and World War II exhibit. The Zeppelin Field, the Congress Hall, and the Documentation Center are included in that one. We won't get back to the boat until six," Kevin said.

"I think that's why we signed up for the shorter one in the afternoon, although yours sound fascinating," Rosetta said.

"You can check to see if the reservation desk has seats available," Tom added.

"That's fine. With the humidity, two hours is all the time I want to spend sightseeing," Rosetta said.

The waiter returned to their table to pour red wine into Rosetta's glass before setting Joyce's cola down. He rounded the table and serviced the other guests their wine.

"I heard the water level has dropped some more," Barbara added. "The program director will tell us tomorrow if we have to change boats."

"What a bother," Kevin remarked.

After dinner, Rosetta and her daughter returned to their cabin for the night.

"You can do something else if you want," Rosetta suggested, reaching for her book off the nightstand.

"No, I'll just catch up on my social sites. Just as well, we are climbing around in an old palace tomorrow."

"Climbing?"

"Yes, the floor had been broken up centuries ago and walking is uneven. You did bring sturdy shoes with you, didn't you?"

"Yes, I did," Rosetta assured her and opened her reader to the last place she had been reading.

"Uh, Joyce, would you rather we go home tomorrow?

"Home? No, I'm not going to let that man have any power over me. Do you want to?" she asked.

"It was a passing thought. You're right. We won't be intimidated."

"That's the mother I know," Joyce said, smiling.

Rosetta smiled in return and opened her reader.

"My dear Katheryn, it has been two weeks since we laid your father in his grave. You really need to think about marrying me to preserve his heritage and all that he had accomplished," said Henry.

The count's daughter, dressed in a satin black dress stared out the narrow window of her father's study.

"What's the hurry, Viceroy?" she asked, turning toward him. "The new customs I've heard in the market are allowing women to own land and businesses."

He licked his lips. Henry didn't want his chance to slip away. *"With the church still powerful, I'll offer her this reason."*

"If you don't marry," he said, "someone from the church would lay claim to the lands. Without the royal ruby to prove your ownership, I'm afraid you will lose everything," he replied.

"I have a confession to make," she said.

"Oh?" he wondered what she was going to say next. He cleared his throat for a different approach. "I have heard you were in love with someone else."

"Yes, but he has vanished. I fear he will never return. You know I can't love you the way I loved my friend."

"Yes, but in time, we shall grow together. I received a letter today from the Pope. He wants to marry us himself."

"Why?"

"We have been friends for a long time. He wants to perform this occasion as a gift from him to us."

"If he feels it's appropriate then I'll marry you," Katheryn resigned.

Later in the afternoon, Henry took a carriage into the village nearby. He gave his coachman, Edward, an order to stop at the local church.

"Here you are, sir. Shall I wait for you?" Edward asked.

"No, I'll meet you at the corner tavern," Henry said.

As soon as the coachman drove his team and carriage down the street, Henry turned and walked to the smithy pounding on his anvil. When the young man noticed the viceroy standing to his right, he stopped his work.

"Good day to you, sir," he said in a loud manner.

"Let's talk inside," Henry said, lowering his voice.

"Come this way. Do you have my gold?" asked the smithy as they strode into the stable.

"Hush! This is all I have for the time being," Viceroy Edmond said, handing over a small sack of coins.

David opened the sack and peered inside. Looking back at the viceroy, he frowned.

"This isn't enough," he said.

"I will have more for you at a later time."

"Then, this is all you get," David said, pulling out a wrapped cloth from his apron.

The viceroy unwrapped the heavy muslin cloth and examined the string of jewels.

"The ruby is missing," he growled.

"Yes, and it will stay missing until you pay me in full," David explained. "I'll give you one week, and then I'll sell it off. After that, I'm heading south."

Henry pocketed the necklace. "Fine, I'll meet you here next week."

That said, he marched out of the smithy's shack and headed toward the tavern. He thought, *"I have to*

167

hide this necklace from Katheryn until we are married. Then she'll appreciate my resourcefulness."

Entering the public house, he ordered a draft of ale. When the barista brought his brew, he wrapped his fingers around the tankard. Taking a long drink, he thought how and when he would break the news of the necklace to his fiancé. Finishing his ale, he walked over to his coachman who played cards at one of the tables.

"Edward, as soon as you finish that hand, I must head for my residence in Bonn," he said.

His coachman finished his game and followed the viceroy outside.

"Bringing a few more things from home, sir?" Edward asked.

"Yes, you know how it is with women," Henry said, climbing into the carriage.

The sun had set by the time the viceroy's coach arrived at his estate.

"Do you want me to help you, sir?" the coachman asked.

"No, find out when a coach leaves for Würzburg," Henry replied and walked into his mansion.

The next morning, Edward approached the viceroy and informed him transportation for the southern city will leave before noon.

"Thank you, Edward. I'm ready to leave now. After you drop me off, return my large bags to Katheryn's home. I'll locate transport back to Cologne."

A. Nation

The journey south took three-days by the time the viceroy arrived at the palace in Würzburg. There he greeted a couple of friends and headed for the temporary lodging he had used in the past.

Glancing around the village square, Henry contemplated what would be the perfect hiding spot for the necklace. He walked down the street when he the local church bells rang from the other end of the street.

Later, arriving back at his palace, he stepped into his study to collect some papers for his upcoming marriage to Katheryn. He rang the call bell. A housekeeper entered the room.

"Yes, sir?" she asked.

"I'll have dinner as soon as it's prepared. Arrange a coach returning to Cologne as soon as possible."

"Right away, Viceroy," she said, bowing and backed out of the room.

Rosetta and Joyce, still in their cabin, heard a special announcement broadcasted through their room's speaker. The program director's voice said there would be a meeting in the lounge this morning to give them an update about the future of their trip. Rosetta turned off her reader before laying it on top of the nightstand. She stood and followed Joyce out the cabin door with everyone else through the narrow hallway. They passed housekeeping personnel and the few officers remaining at the reception desk.

Rosetta leaned over and spoke in a hushed voice.

"You didn't elaborate, but was there a good-looking young man with curly black hair with your captors?" Rosetta asked, climbing the stairs.

"No, just ugly fat men. Why?"

"I'm trying to figure out how the young man I saw at the airport and the vendor market is involved with the key and the diary," Rosetta said.

"You know, I really don't care if we ever find out," Joyce said, stepping to the top step of the second deck. "I just want to forget the whole mess with those people."

"I understand. Are you sure, you want to go on this next tour? It's part of our package, so you don't have to," Rosetta asked.

"As long as we stay together with the group, we should be all right," Joyce replied. "I'm not going to let those people have power over me."

"That's the strong girl I raised," Rosetta said.

They walked through the crowd of passengers and found a couple of empty seats near the bow. The program director started his announcement.

"Glad all of you could make it. I will inform you now that our water level is drastically low in the canal. So we are making the decision to bus you to our sister ship on the Rhine River. It is an identical boat to this one. Your room numbers will stay the same, and those of you on a tour, your bus driver shall divert from his schedule to meet the other boat. All we ask of you is to have your luggage packed and placed outside your door by 4:00 a.m. We will load your bags on a transport truck so you don't have to worry about them. Make sure you check your room safes and clean those out as well. Keep your personal items with you in a carry-on. That is all. Enjoy your lunch," he said.

"Been there, done that," Rosetta murmured.

Several people left the room. Rosetta rose up and as soon as Joyce began to follow her out of the lounge, the program director approached them.

"I hope, madams, you are enjoying your trip with us," he said.

"Yes, we are. Oh, did you return that little book back to the museum all right?" Rosetta asked.

"Little black book, Oh, yes, yes, uh, make sure you take your valuables and receivers with you on your tour," he urged.

"Thank you, bye."

Rosetta headed for the stairway when Joyce leaned over to her.

"Why did he ask about our valuables? Did he think we didn't hear his speech during the announcement?" she asked.

"Who knows. Maybe he is just concerned."

"And he didn't act like he was aware of your little book, either," Joyce said.

"He's a busy man. But that did seem odd."

As soon as the two women stepped off the stairway, they headed into the dining room.

After lunch, they retrieved their tour cards and headed out to their waiting bus. On the gangway, they watched men loading lots of luggage into the back of a semi-trailer truck. Tom waved at Rosetta and walked over.

"Are you going with us on this tour, Tom?" Rosetta asked.

"Nope, I signed up for the tour Barbara talked about last night at dinner. I just wanted to see you off. You two have a nice day," he said, waving as he walked back to his bus.

"Thanks," Rosetta said and headed for their tour bus.

They settled into their seats and the bus drove down the street.

Joyce leaned over and whispered, "Where did you hide that necklace and key?"

"I'm not telling," Rosetta said, staring down the aisle.

"Why?"

"Best you don't know," Rosetta said. Speaking louder, "Oh, would you look at that lion statue."

Joyce laughed and gave her historical input. "Lions are popular symbols of strength. My travel book said you will find them in front of cafes, buildings, or beer gardens."

"If we see a beer garden, I'll treat you," Rosetta said, smiling.

"Yeah, I was told by my contact they were touring the old castle today. You are? But I'm sure—very well," Alfredo said before he disconnected his call.

"Mario!" he shouted.

"Yeah, boss," Mario said, entering the room.

"Get my car. We're taking a trip."

The bus tour took Rosetta and Joyce up the steep roadway until it stopped on a graveled pathway not far from the castle ruins. Rosetta and Joyce followed their tour mates out of the bus, connected with their guide, and turned on their receivers. Rosetta noticed his muscular legs and arms.

"He must do this every day," she said to Joyce.

In his thick Swiss accent, their guide said, "Many famous people have come from Wertheim. To name a few, Albert Einstein, Sophie Scholl who was a member of the Nazi resistance, and Boris Becker, the tennis player, to name a few."

They strolled by a tall brick structure with a round pointed roof.

"In this tower, the citizens used to house drunkards or women who argued a lot, sometimes as long as thirty days. Notice how it leans a little. This is due to the water level, not a construction defect. Now over here…"

Joyce stopped to take a picture before they entered the castle grounds. Rosetta waited until Joyce finished before they continued their walk behind the tour group.

"Most of the ornate rooms had been destroyed in the seventeenth century by gunpowder," their guide added.

The floor had sizeable masonry and boulders scattered about. Large slabs of cement and stucco had fallen down from the walls, creating a stair step shape to the next level of the castle. Rosetta stopped to change the battery in her camera. Joyce waited nearby.

"Look, Mom, a restored room. Let's take a look."

"We should stay with the tour group," Rosetta said, peering inside the empty room.

Joyce noticed a large man step behind them. Before she could step aside to let him pass, he shoved both of them inside the stark room and drew his gun. Stumbling over the stone slabs, Joyce held on to her mother, preventing her from falling onto the hard stone surface.

Chapter 18 - Aric

"What do you want of us?" Rosetta asked, regaining her balance. Joyce still held onto her mother's arm.

Before the man could answer, a plumpish man in a khaki suit and hat appeared around the corner of the arch in the stone wall.

"That's the man, Mom," Joyce said, pointing at Alfredo.

Realizing Joyce identified the man who struck her daughter, she attempted to lash out in anger. Before she could, another man and a woman step out from behind the overweight man.

"Mr. Heyburn, Mary, what are you doing here?" Rosetta exclaimed when she saw them.

"You know why, don't you, Mrs. Blessing?" Alfredo asked.

"Mr. Heyburn? Mary?" Rosetta asked.

Mary's distinctive swagger approached the two women.

"The name ain't Mary, it's Gloria Montaign," she corrected with a snap of the gum in her mouth.

Mr. Heyburn said, "I'm sorry, Rosetta, but when Harry Brown died, I needed someone else to transport the diary to Alfredo. But you almost messed that up when you took your daughter instead of Gloria. When you handed over the book to my contact on your boat, we realized we needed the old key."

"Look, I can give you the necklace, it's worth something. It's locked in my safe on the boat," Rosetta lied.

"No, it isn't. My contact already broke into your safe," said Alfredo. "That means the necklace has to be either in your totes or on your person. Do I have to order Gloria to search you in front of us?" he asked.

"No, just a minute," Rosetta said, reaching under her blouse.

Joyce stood in front of her and whispered, "Mom, don't give it to them."

"We have to," she replied, pulling out the strand of jewels. "It's not worth our lives if they have weapons."

Gloria grabbed the necklace.

"Hey, there's a stone missing," she cried, holding the strand in the air.

"Give that to me," Alfredo said, grabbing the necklace from her hand.

"Where is it, Rosetta?" Mr. Heyburn asked, raising his voice and stepping closer to her.

"I found it like that," Joyce volunteered.

"Where is the ruby?" yelled Alfredo, who rushed at the two women.

"Stand where you are and back away," shouted an unfamiliar male voice from behind Gloria.

He held a gun on Alfredo, Heyburn, and Gloria. Rosetta recognized him as the young man from the airport lounge.

"Everyone, move over there. You too, big guy," he said, shaking the barrel of his pistol at the man guarding the arch. "Madams, stay where you are."

He jerked the strand of jewels away from Gloria's hand, pocketed them, and backed away toward the archway.

"Who are you? And you speak English," Rosetta asked.

"A friend. I'll allow you two to step back outside. I'll catch up with you while I hold these people off," he said.

Rosetta and Joyce didn't waste any time hurrying out under the stone archway. Just as their tour group passed them heading for their tour bus, they merged with several people and walked out of the castle.

"Shall we wait for him?" Joyce asked, glancing in back of the tour assembly.

"No, let's find our bus. Maybe we'll see him—," Rosetta started to say.

"Keep moving ladies, I'm right behind you," they heard their benefactor say behind them.

"Who are you?" Joyce whispered back.

"Aric. Hurry."

Walking fast on gravel began to hurt Rosetta's ankles. Joyce held onto her. Approaching the bus, they climb onboard. The tall young man followed them inside.

Joyce and Rosetta found their seats toward the rear of the bus. Their new friend flashed his ID to the bus driver and followed Rosetta. He slid into the seat behind them.

"How come our guide let you on the bus?" Rosetta asked.

"I have special privileges. Before we get to your boat, I'll tell you as much as I can," he whispered behind them.

Their bus ride brought the passengers through the city, passing statues of famous heroes and religious leaders. Turning down the long port side of the river, their bus pulled up next to the gangway of their riverboat. Once they were outside of the bus, Aric motioned them over to a metal park bench under a few trees. The humid heat of the day compared to the air conditioning of the bus, made Rosetta grateful for the shade.

"Ladies," he gestured toward the bench.

"Now, who are you?" Joyce asked.

"I am Aric Richter. I'm an unofficial count. My many great grandfathers ago from the fifteenth century used to own all this," he said, sweeping his arm around.

"When my ancient relative died, all his heirs were deprived of their inheritance once his daughter married the viceroy."

"Just like in my book. I'm sorry but I have been reading a fictional account of that time period. Do go on," Rosetta said.

"With the death of the count, our valuable jewels were stolen as well. Did you tell the truth about the missing ruby?" he asked Joyce.

"Yes, I found the necklace in a building air vent when I escaped from Mr. Fat Guy."

"You were lucky. We believe he has killed many people searching for that necklace."

"Who's 'we'?" Joyce asked.

"Now and then, I work for Interpol." He reached into his jacket pocket, flashed his I.D. card, and shoved it back into his pants.

"But what about those people? They'll come after us," Rosetta asked, wiping the sweat from her forehead.

"I have called the local police to pick them up."

"I'd feel better if you would make sure they have before we get on the boat," Rosetta said, rising from the bench.

At that moment, the man's phone beeped.

"One moment, please. I have to take this call," he said, answering his cell phone.

Rosetta could just make out what he was saying on his phone.

"Good, excellent. Oh, he did, did he? Well, I'm not surprised. I will keep on watch. Goodbye."

He walked back to both women under the shade.

"Everyone, including the Americans, has been picked up but Alfredo and his henchman. It is safe for you to board your ship," Aric said.

"Thank you. Sorry, we couldn't find the ruby for you," Rosetta said, shaking his hand.

"Yes, thank you," Joyce added.

"Wait. Let me give you my phone number in case you need to contact me," he said.

Aric pulled out a small business card and handed it to Joyce. Accepting the card with his Interpol insignia, she thanked him. The two women walked toward the gangway. Arriving at the registration desk, they dropped off their tour cards and headed for their cabin.

"Oh, I forgot to give him the key," exclaimed Rosetta just as they entered their room.

"Save it as a souvenir. I'm showering first," Joyce said.

"I should call him and if he's still around, we can give it to him later," Rosetta said.

"Mom, are you trying to fix me up with the count?"

"Count in name only. I thought you liked him?"

"Call if you want. I'm showering first," Joyce replied and took off for their bathroom.

Rosetta dialed the phone number. As soon as Aric's voice mail came on, she left a message.

"I forgot to give you the key. Let me know where we can meet," she recorded.

Their boat sailed passed Lahnstein, Vallendar, and Neuweid. Each town displayed their name on a large white billboard along the banks of the Rhine. Their next stop would be Cologne or Köln as the Germans spell the name. Rosetta noticed the boat was sailing through the night when they finished dinner. Walking back to their room, the

Program Director at the reception desk asked how their day had been.

"Just fine," Rosetta answered in passing.

"Does that man smile too much or is it me?" Joyce asked, following her mother down the narrow hallway.

"That's his job," Rosetta replied as she unlocked her door.

"Maybe so, but I guess I don't trust him after all we've been through."

"Look most of the bad guys were caught, we know Aric is on what's his name's trail, and as soon as he calls me back, we can get rid of this key in my tote."

"This is one adventure I'll never forget. Is the boat sailing all night?" Joyce asked, undressing for bed.

"Yes, we dock in Cologne tomorrow according to today's newsletter. Oh, it says there's a special meeting in the lounge before dinner to update us on the water level and the rest of our trip," Rosetta said. "Our tour for the Cologne walking tour is tomorrow after breakfast at 9:30 a.m. and we'll see the Great Saint Martin's church in the Old Town district."

Rosetta set down the two-page paper on the counter in front of their beds.

"Do you have any ideas from your book where that key belongs?" Joyce asked.

"It could be for the wooden box or the chest of drawers. I had hoped we would have found out by now. I'll read some more tonight. It's an interesting story," Rosetta said, heading for the restroom to wash.

Chapter 19 – Cologne Church

The next morning, Rosetta and her daughter dressed for their walking tour and headed for breakfast carrying their tote bags.

"Oh, I forgot my receiver, I'll meet you at the table," Rosetta said, turning to walk back to their cabin.

"I'll see if Tom is in the dining room," Joyce replied and continued walking.

Rosetta unlocked her cabin door and picked up her receiver. Placing the long strap around her neck, she looked over at the nightstand. Deciding to take her reader with her, she walked over to the nightstand between the beds and placed it into her tote.

"Maybe there is something else I might read about this key," she mumbled to herself.

She locked the door on her way out and strolled down the hallway toward the dining room. Hans, the Program Director, wished her a good morning. He sat behind the reception desk looking at the computer reservation screen. Rosetta smiled and marched on.

Glancing around the dining room, she spotted her daughter and Tom sitting at one of the tables. Rosetta noticed an empty chair between Tom and her daughter.

A waiter approached their table, holding menus in one hand.

A. Nation

"Buffet or from the menu this morning, madam?" he asked.

"I'll just do the buffet, thank you," Rosetta replied. Turning to her friend, "Well, Tom, are you joining us today?"

"If you are seeing the Cologne Cathedral today, I am," he replied.

"I heard it's pretty big," she said.

"Yes, the main tower is 157 meters high or 515 feet," Tom said, sipping some of his water.

The waiter set down their orange juice.

"I ordered the OJ for you, Mom. You can get coffee later if you want," Joyce said.

"Thank you. It's just what I need," Rosetta replied and nodded to the waiter when he set it by her glass of water.

Tom continued on about the church.

"The church was built on a Roman foundation after a fire in the early twelfth century," Tom continued.

"I hope we can go inside. It must be beautiful," Rosetta said.

"That it is. The church has high ceilings and lovely stained glass windows," Tom replied.

"How do you know so much about the church," Joyce asked.

"My late wife and I visited it many years ago in our younger days. My memory isn't so good anymore so when this trip came up, I wanted to see it again."

Tom had ordered from the menu. As soon as his meal arrived, Rosetta and Joyce rose from their chairs to walk over to the buffet. Joyce chose several pieces of fruit and an apple after she had scooped some scrambled eggs on her plate.

"Are you eating all that?" Rosetta asked.

"I thought I'd eat the apple later," Joyce replied.

Rosetta picked up the tongs by the pastries and chose an apple fritter, red browned potatoes, sausages, and some fruit.

Noticing her daughter had only fruit and eggs on her plate, "Are you sure that's all you are going to eat this morning?" she asked Joyce.

"This is it. I ate too much last night at dinner," Joyce replied.

"No wonder you're so skinny," Rosetta said.

"Love you too, Mom."

They returned to their table to rejoin Tom and another couple that had sat down. Rosetta noticed the man's accent sounded like he came from New York. Relaying their previous experiences from home in the states, Rosetta looked at her watch.

"Well, we better get a move on. Our tour bus should be ready soon," Rosetta said.

Joyce dropped her apple into her tote bag. Rosetta, Tom, and Joyce rose from their chairs and said goodbye to their table friends. Making their way to the reception area, they turned left. The sliding glass door opened. They each chose a water bottle from the table outside the exit. Rosetta placed her unsealed bottle of water into her tote and hefted the straps over her shoulder.

Joyce noticing the full tote, asked, "Mom, why is your bag so bulky looking?"

"I thought I'd bring my reader and read it on the bus. There might be a reference where the key would be used."

Joyce sighed. "Okay, if it gets too heavy for you, I'll carry your water bottle."

"No need. It's not that heavy," Rosetta assured.

A. Nation

They walked through the gangway toward their tour bus. On the ground, they could see crewmen unloading their luggage from the back of a container truck.

"Oh look, I see Tom waiting for us," Joyce said and waved.

Once inside their bus, Rosetta let Joyce have the window seat again. As she sat next to her, Tom found an empty seat behind them.

"Ladies and gentlemen, your guide will meet you when I stop at the church square," their driver said.

Tom leaned over. "It's a beautiful day today," he said.

Rosetta nodded and pulled out her reader.

Viceroy Henry Edmond and his new lovely wife, Katheryn, had wedded in the largest church of the civilized world. Cologne's beauty of flowering trees and spring flowers circled the grounds of the five-spired basilica. Inside rose fourteen pillars adorned with statues from the church's past. Grand stained windows let the colorful sunlight flow across the floor.

The loyal town's people treated their new lord and his wife to a reception on the grassy grounds behind the church. After much hand shaking from the populace, Henry watched Katheryn stop to talk to a few women. Stepping back into the church, he set to climbing the stairs to the second level where the rooms of the clergy slept. The stairs twisted and turned until he reached a landing. Another few steps and he turned down the long hallway toward a small room located on his left. He pulled out a large metal

183

key from his waistcoat and inserted it into the door's lock. Henry opened the door to survey the small room.

There to the right of the bed sat the old count's bureau he had donated. The sun streamed through the small window on the opposite wall. After making final arrangements with the smithy near Katheryn's home, he had placed a small box in the top drawer. Opening the wooden drawer, he lifted the dark-colored box out and set it on the bed. The wooden box, now darkened with age had painted pansies decorated on the cover. The container held the one item he could use to win Katheryn's heart forever.

Pocketing the key back into his jacket, he opened the lid of the dark colored box. Reaching into a swath of shiny cloth, he unfolded the maroon satin to admire the single five-carat ruby nestled inside. Then he returned the jewel back into the fabric folds, closed the lid of the box, and tucked it under his arm. Satisfied, he headed back downstairs.

As he approached the winding staircase, he heard footsteps marching up the stairs. He knew if the residing order found him with this jewel, they would claim it for the church. A monk rounded the hallway far behind him. Returning to the room, he ducked inside and held his breath. *"What if they find me? What if they take my box?"* he asked himself, turning the door latch with care.

He groped the cold cement wall behind him in the dark. This room's window faced away from the sun's bright light. As he moved his hand over the wall to feel his surroundings, his hands moved a loose stone. Peeling the smooth rock away, he inserted his arm to feel the depth of the cavity. Footsteps sounded closer. He stuffed the small black box inside the wall and rushed to replace the stone. Still holding the key, he threw it through the open window into the grassy brush below by the church wall. He waited until the footsteps faded.

The tour bus came to a stop and expelled the hydraulic air from the engine. Rosetta turned off her reader and returned it to her tote. They exited through the side door of the bus, hurrying over to meet their guide waiting nearby on the cement steps in front of the gigantic church.

Everyone tapped their guide's transmitter paddle to hear him speak.

"Thank you, everyone, for coming. We will walk through the church. You may look around for ten minutes. Please do not disturb the worshippers. Come this way."

Rosetta bent her head upward trying to see the tall steeples. *"There's no way, I can take a decent picture of this,"* she thought, following the tour group into the basilica.

As she walked through the enormous doors, she noticed a stone stairway to her left, blocked off with construction wood horses. She went to look at it but couldn't proceed any further due to the barrier in front of the stairway.

"You'd like to go up there, wouldn't you?" Joyce whispered in her ear.

"This is the stairway described in my book. It twists around and goes up to the second floor. The author thought the viceroy hid something in one of the rooms," Rosetta said.

"But it's a fictional book."

"Yes, but it's based on real events," Rosetta explained. "The author had studied this tale for some time."

Joyce pulled her mother toward the back center of the cathedral. Upward their eyes adjusted to the poor light. The gothic ceiling arched over them at a great height.

"Look, Mom, the stained glass is beautiful," Joyce remarked, taking a couple of pictures.

The tour flowed out of the other church entrance and into the street.

"As you can see, some construction is still continuing on the façade," their guide remarked. "The workers have cleaned that side of the stonework. Can you see the difference? The dark-toned side still has to be washed."

They walked on in the humid heat, crossing the cobblestone roadway. Joyce had a hard time stepping across the stones due to her short feet. They passed a dry fountain under repair with a statue of a young woman holding a lamp. The plaque on the side told of the story how she watches over the elves of Cologne who work in the salt mines through the night.

"Reminds me of Snow White and the dwarves. Do you suppose that's where the story came from?" Joyce asked.

"Could be, the similarity to the two stories is uncanny," Rosetta remarked, waving her hand to cool herself in the morning heat.

"Here, Mom. Take my battery fan."

"Thank you. I've noticed there are breweries on every corner. Let's get a cold one at lunchtime," she said, turning on the small fan.

They walked down by the river and toward the chocolate factory. The guide told everyone they had free time and to meet at the church to catch a bus back to the boat.

"The buses leave at regular intervals until six o'clock at night," he said.

"Mom, let's see what the chocolate place has," Joyce asked.

They walked about two miles before coming to the entrance of the chocolate museum. After they paid by the gift store, they walked upstairs to the museum. Many of the metal twelve-inch molds were for chocolate animals and Christmas motifs that sat in glass cases. The plastic molds hung across the ceiling reflecting the sunlight.

Rosetta and her daughter stood in line for a free sample from the chocolate fountain and the large gold replica of a chocolate bean tree. Returning to the first floor, they entered the gift shop.

"Can we take some home?" Joyce asked.

"Yes, it's just meat and produce products we can't take."

Selecting their choices, they headed outside to return to the church and their waiting bus. Rosetta hadn't realized how far they walked from the church square. Over cobblestones which were set wide apart, and enduring the hot air, they stopped at a corner outdoor brewery. Joyce ordered two cold beers while Rosetta adjusted her bags near her chair. The waitress, dressed in a Swiss costume, brought their drinks to their table. Rosetta paid the girl.

"I never appreciated beer this much as I do now," Rosetta said, drinking in a few gulps.

"I'm with you, Mom. This hits the spot."

"And is this spot taken?" said a male voice.

They looked up and recognized Aric.

"Please sit down. Do you want a beer?" Rosetta asked.

"No, thank you. I'm fine. Did you bring the key?" he asked.

"Yes, but it's at the bottom of my tote," she said.

"No problem. When you finish your beers, I'll walk back with you to the church. That's where we will need the key," he said.

"Thank you. Oh, there's a friend of mine. I'll leave you two for a moment and see if he wants to join us," Rosetta said, taking another sip of her beer before she left their table.

She left her bag with Joyce and hurried over to meet with Tom. He was glancing around the tables when he saw her waving him over. They sat down at the next table near Joyce and Aric. Rosetta wanted the two younger people to get to know each other better. *"Granted he's not a wealthy count, but he is somebody of importance in this country,"* she thought.

"I see you have been shopping," Tom said, taking a seat.

The waitress took his order.

"Yes, we loaded up at the chocolate factory. And you?"

"I just bought a little souvenir magnet for my fridge. I don't have a lot of room back home for knickknacks anymore," he replied.

They talked a while about his home in Ohio. Rosetta glanced over and noticed Joyce had gathered their tote bags.

"I know what you mean. It looks like my daughter is ready to leave. We are heading back to the church before we catch a bus," Rosetta explained.

The waitress brought his order and Tom paid her with a large bill.

"I'll meet you at the church," Tom said, clasping his hands around his cool glass of beer.

Rosetta stood and followed her daughter and Aric. The young man looked at her and nodded. They walked another mile and a half through tour groups and visiting families until they arrived at the Cologne Church. The flow of tourists had decreased, as they entered the main doors.

"Madam, your key?" Aric said, holding his hand out.

Rosetta fished around in her tote, brought up the rusty metal key, and handed it over to him. *"Maybe he knows where the ruby is,"* she thought.

"I believe I know where to use the key upstairs," he said, "After you, ladies."

"Oh, you go Joyce. I'm going to sit down for a spell. All that walking in the heat wears me out."

She wasn't worried about Aric since he showed us his Interpol I.D. *"Joyce should be safe enough with him,"* she thought.

"Okay, we'll be right down," Joyce said and followed Aric up the stone steps.

Rosetta watched as the two turned and climbed the stairway. *"I'll give them some time alone,"* she mused, reaching into her tote to read a few more pages from her reader.

After a pair of monks strode by the doorway, he ran down the stairs and out onto the grounds. While he searched the clump of bushes by the church walls, someone approached him from behind. He straightened to face one of the Cardinals.

"Oh, there you are, Viceroy, come, we are starting the feast."

"Thank you, but I will see you in a moment," Henry replied.

"Oh, that can wait, come with me and I will toast your new marriage to the countess," the cardinal insisted, encircling his arm around Henry's shoulders. Henry smiled at the cardinal.

"So, where are you and your mother from?" Aric asked.

"Washington" she replied and added "—D.C. She manages a travel agency there. That's how come we got such a good deal on our tickets."

They arrived at the top of the winding stairs and strolled through the hallway.

"Is Washington this warm at this time of year?"

"It's humid, but not this hot," Joyce replied.

"I think it's in this room," he said, gesturing toward a dark wooden door.

He tried to open the door but found it locked. Joyce watched him as he inserted the old key into the keyhole. With a click, they smiled at each other when the door latch released.

"I think this door has been locked for centuries," Aric said.

"Smells like it too," Joyce added as she stepped inside the small room.

Chapter 20 - Discovery

Rosetta read a few more pages from her reader.

He glanced back at the clump of bushes and smiled. *"I'll have to get the key later,"* he thought.

The joyous party continued well into the night. Many out-of-town guests found rooms to bed down in the church or the castle nearby. The next morning, Henry rose before dawn. He slipped out of bed, taking care not to waken Katheryn. After he dressed, he left their bedchamber and hurried outside.

He searched for the key through the bushes until the sun rose over the mountains. He couldn't find the key. "What if someone found it?" he worried.

"Viceroy, have you lost something?" a voice said behind him.

He turned around and discovered one of the groundskeepers looking at him.

"Uh, yes. It's not important. I can get another. In the festival last night, I thought my scarf flew over here in the breeze last night," he lied.

"If I find it, sir, I'll make sure it is washed and returned to you," the serf said.

"Thank you. I must be on my way," Henry said and walked away from the grounds keeper.

Rosetta was about to nod off until her eye came upon pictures of the old count's family. The first ones were copies of paintings done in the earlier centuries. Further down the hallway came the later portraits in black and white photos. A woman rounded the pew from her tour group and sat down near her.

"Rosetta, isn't it?" she asked.

"Yes, I'm waiting for my daughter. We've just returned from the chocolate factory."

"How was it? I wanted to go, but that's too far for me to walk."

"Very interesting," Rosetta replied. "We bought some, of course."

"If you don't mind, I need to say a prayer," the woman said, sitting near to Rosetta on the wooden pew.

Rosetta nodded and returned to her reading. Scanning the next page, she gazed upon a photo of an older man. When she read the caption, she jerked off the pew bench, startling the woman sitting next to her.

"I'm sorry, please watch my bags. I have an emergency," Rosetta said, holding onto her reader. She rushed over to the stone stairway.

Pulling the barrier away, she dashed up the spiral staircase as fast as she could. She ran down the hallway, checking each door. She tried one door that was unlocked. There stood a priest half-dressed.

"Oh, so sorry," she said and shut the door to continue on her quest.

She found a few more doors locked. Then the last one opened. Joyce and Aric stood over a black box on the metal framed bed.

"Mom, he found it!" Joyce exclaimed. "What's wrong? You look out of breath."

"That's great news," Rosetta said, breathing hard. "Joyce, would you mind coming over here for a minute?"

"Did you think we were doing something else?" Joyce asked, smiling.

"Please come here, Joyce," Rosetta asked again a little stronger.

"All right. What is it, Mom?" she asked, moving closer to her mother.

Rosetta pulled her closer to the doorway and called back to the young man.

"Aric, or whatever your name is, just take the jewel and leave us."

"Mom?"

"Honey, this is not Aric Richter. The real Mr. Richter is eighty-two years old and lives in Italy. He has only two daughters and no heirs, see," Rosetta explained, showing her the photo on her reader.

"Aric?" Joyce asked, turning to look at him.

"Ah, yes, he is my grandfather. He has disowned me," the false Aric said.

Rosetta said, trying to back into the hallway. "Your voice. I remember now. You were in that church where I heard two men fighting. We are leaving now."

"No, I think not," he said, gesturing them to come back inside.

"But you told us you were with Interpol," Joyce said.

"Well, in a way I am. They just have to find me. Please ladies, over here," he beckoned.

When they didn't move inside the room, he pulled out his small pistol and motioned them to sit on each side of the bed frame. He closed the small black box and inserted it into a pocket within his jacket. After shutting the door, he pulled out a thin rope and ordered Rosetta to tie Joyce's wrists on the metal rail at the end of the bed.

"Sorry, madam, but you know too much," he said.

"But I trusted you," Joyce yelled.

"Unfortunate, but necessary."

"You can't leave us here," Rosetta shot back in anger. "The police will find you."

You madam, sit with your back to your daughter. Don't worry, I'll leave the door unlocked. Someone is bound to hear you," he said. "And as for the police, that's a chance I'm willing to take."

Rosetta turned and allowed him to tie her arms to the railing. Just as he was struggling to tie a knot, the door flung open. Rosetta's jaw dropped when she saw who had burst through the door. The other man also had a gun in his hand.

"Put it down, Marco," said the boat's program director, pointing his gun. "I work for Interpol, ladies. We have been tracking this man for two years across Europe."

Aric or Marco placed the flat side of the gun on the floor, still holding onto a thin piece of rope in his other hand.

"Ah, Hans, good to see you again," Marco said, grinning as he rose to stand before the boat officer.

"Untie these women," Hans ordered the fake Aric.

"And how do we know that? This man had an I.D. that looked authentic," Rosetta said, wiggling her wrists in the loose tie.

"Looked authentic is the word," Hans said, moving toward them. With his gun on Marco, he pulled out his I.D. from his shirt pocket with his other hand. "Here is what it should look like." The I.D. card in his holder shined back with the gold imprinting and a fingerprint.

Marco dropped his free hand and flung the loose cord at Hans. Rosetta noticed Joyce's apple had rolled out of her bag and stopped at her feet.

"He has the jewel," Rosetta blurted out and freed her hands from the loose tie. She picked up the apple and threw it at Marco's head.

Marco tried to sprint into the hallway. When Hans raised his hands as the rope whipped at his face, he reached out and grabbed Marco's shirt. They both fell brawling on the floor. Marco twisted around and scurried out the door. Hans stood up and gave chase.

When the scuffle played out on the floor, Rosetta untied Joyce from the bed railing. Joyce wrung the pain left by the tightrope and stood up.

"Thank goodness you got to me in time," she said to Rosetta.

"When I saw that photo of the authentic Aric Richter on the page and his history, I just took off up those stairs. Darn if I was going to leave you alone with this Marco character. What a smoothie. He had me convinced as well."

"Thanks, Mom. Why is it every time I like a guy, he turns out to be the bad boy?" Joyce asked, following her mother toward the hallway.

"Must be in our genes. Let's get out of here," Rosetta said, placing her hand around Joyce's waist.

As they navigated down the winding staircase, there was Tom standing at the bottom.

"Are you ladies all right?" he asked with one hand leaning against the stone wall.

"Yes, have you seen Hans, our program director?" Rosetta asked.

"Yes, he and that young fella came down a few minutes ago. I was worried that you hadn't arrived at the bus so I walked back, thinking you were still here. That young man, Aric, flew at me, and we tumbled to the floor. Hans grabbed him by his arm and handcuffed him right there in front of me. This nice lady helped me up," he said, gesturing to the woman who Rosetta had left her bags on the pew.

"Oh, thank you," Rosetta said to the lady. "And I'm glad you're all right, Tom."

"A little bruised, but okay. Say, something fell out of Aric's jacket," Tom said, holding a black box in his hands.

"The ruby!" Joyce exclaimed.

Tom pulled up the tiny latch and unfolded the red satin cloth inside. There in the center laid the large ruby.

"Well, I'll be. What shall we do with this?" he asked.

"Give it to me," Rosetta said. "I intend to take it to the police tomorrow."

"But you could give it to Hans, he'll return it to its rightful owner," Joyce suggested.

"Hmm, I have a better idea. Let's get on our bus and we'll discuss it on the way back to the boat," Tom said, handing the black box to Rosetta.

Slipping the container with its precious commodity into her tote bag, they walked outside toward their waiting bus. After locating seats where they could sit close to each other, Tom and Rosetta discussed the possibilities of what to do with the red ruby. Joyce sat behind them, leaning over the back of the chairs. Deciding on a plan, they discovered they had just arrived at the boat dock.

"Meet me at dinnertime?" Tom asked.

"We will," Rosetta answered.

As they walked into the boat, Rosetta and Joyce noticed the Program Director was absent from the reservation desk.

"Must have Interpol work to do," Joyce said.

"No matter. I like Tom's idea and will find out if he's made the call by dinnertime," Rosetta said.

When they arrived at their cabin, Rosetta inserted the small black box into their replaced safe and locked the security door.

"We have two hours. Let's enjoy our balcony," Joyce suggested, pulling out a deck of cards from her suitcase.

"We have to leave early to hear where our trip will go tomorrow. I heard some of the crew mentioned the water level is too low," Rosetta said.

They washed up and Rosetta showed Joyce the picture of the real Aric Richter again.

"Do you still miss the fake Aric?" Rosetta asked.

"No, I feel betrayed. He was so nice to me," Joyce replied.

"I know. Someday you'll meet a nice young man and forget all about Marco."

"No, Mom, I don't think I will. He seemed—so adventurous," she said.

"File it away in your good memories. I did that with your father after he left us."

They sat outside on the balcony watching tourists picnic on shore and the speedboats cruising by.

"Oh, Mom, will you look at that," Joyce said, pointing at a man sitting with his bare back to them on the bow of the small speedboat.

"Joyce, he doesn't have a stitch on him," Rosetta said, raising her eyebrows. "I bet he'll get a good sunburn."

"Who cares, this is the best view I've seen on our entire trip," Joyce laughed.

Laughing along with her daughter, Rosetta had to agree.

They passed the time playing cards until dinnertime. Dressed in their best clothes, they walked to the lounge upstairs. The captain was standing at the microphone, waiting for passengers to fill up the lounge. Rosetta walked in and they found seats by the large glass window.

"Ladies and gentlemen, may I have your attention. Our program director, Hans, has been delayed so I will fill you in what we are doing tomorrow. When we arrived in Cologne today, we barely floated in by ten centimeters or three inches to you Americans."

Some passengers gasped.

"So tonight, you need to pack your luggage that you don't mind missing for a day. You will go on your scheduled tours to the windmills and afterward, your bus will take you to Amsterdam. We have booked hotel rooms for all of you. Transportation has been arranged for you for the next morning to the airport so you won't be late for your plane. Any questions?"

"Do we bring our receivers?" somebody asked.

"Yes, if you have a tour scheduled, please bring them. A steward will pick up the chargers in the morning. After your tour, you'll turn them over to your guide or our program director."

A few people raised their hands and the captain clarified what he had just stated. With the announcement over, Rosetta and Joyce headed downstairs to the dining room. Locating a table, Tom caught up with them and sat down near Rosetta.

"Good news. The real Mr. Richter is flying into Amsterdam and will meet us before we fly out," he relayed.

"That's great. This sure has been an odd day," Rosetta said, looking over the menu the waiter had handed her.

"Mom had his picture in her book. That's how she saved me at the church," Joyce added. "I suppose we could've walked away from him, but we'll never know, will we?"

After dinner, they packed their large suitcase and left it outside their doors. Dressed in pajamas, Joyce pulled out two packages of hot chocolate and poured the contents into their ceramic cups sitting on a silver tray.

"Thank you, dear," Rosetta said, grasping the cup's bottom and handle.

The phone in their room rang. Rosetta looked at Joyce. Joyce shrugged. Rosetta reached for the receiver.

"Yes?"

"Mrs. Blessing?"

"Yes, that' me."

"This is Hans, your program director."

"Oh, yes, what can I do for you?"

"The small metal box the thief had. Did you pick it up by chance?"

"Yes, I have it safe and sound here."

"I could have someone come and relieve you of it."

"We already made arrangements with the true owner. You are welcome to come with us when we go to the Amsterdam airport to meet him."

"Yes, I would like that."

"Good we'll see you day after tomorrow," Rosetta said.

When Hans hung up, Rosetta did the same.

"Good going, Mom," Joyce said.

"Well, how would I know if the man he sends is trustworthy? I don't even know if I just talked to Hans except for the distinctive accent of his."

"Hey, here's a good movie on tonight," Joyce said, reading the TV menu.

"Good but no murder mysteries. I'm storied out."

Chapter 21 - Windmills

In the morning, they once again collected their personal items and filled their tote bags. Rosetta took the jewel and secured it into her passport purse under her blouse. She then placed the empty black box into her tote bag. They walked out of the cabin and met Tom for breakfast. Within the next hour, they climb onboard their tour bus. Rosetta noticed there was another driver sitting across from the man at the steering wheel.

"Two drivers?" she asked.

"Yes," their guide said. "We allow our bus drivers to drive only for two hours. Amsterdam is four hours away, so when we stop for a break, they will change off. It's our law for safety."

Satisfied with her answer, they found seats toward the back of the bus. Tom sat across from Rosetta by the aisle.

Rosetta leaned over and asked Tom, "Have you seen these windmills before?"

"No, this will be a first for me. I've always wanted to see what was inside of them. Oh, I just received a call from Mr. Richter. He's excited to meet you."

"I bet he is. Oh, here's his picture."

Rosetta pulled out her reader and opened it to the page of photos.

"This man here," she said, pointing to the real Aric Richter.

Tom nodded and eased back into his seat. The bus began moving. A couple of hours passed. Rosetta had fallen asleep before the bus pulled to a stop at a convenience store and a fast food franchise.

"Are we there already?" she asked, opening her eyes.

"Just a bathroom break, Mom," Joyce replied.

Their guide spoke to the passengers over the intercom system. "We will take a half hour break here to use the facilities and our drivers will switch. You can leave your bags on the bus. Our driver will lock the doors until he is ready to drive on. Please be quick, everyone."

"I'm going to get a granola bar. I'm all out."

"I'm taking my passport purse with me. I trust no one to leave it here with the ruby inside," Rosetta said, touching the thin strap around her neck. She patted the small bag resting under her blouse for assurance. Grabbing the handle of the seat in front of her, she pulled herself up.

Over a hundred and seventy passengers exited their buses and entered one at a time into the large hamburger franchise. Many bought snack and drinks. Rosetta and Joyce returned to their bus and climbed back on board. The bus drive took another two hours. Soon, the windmills came into view.

"Mom, this is so exciting. Real windmills," Joyce exclaimed, looking out her window.

Rosetta beamed. The response brought back memories of her little girl again, surprised at all that was new.

The tour bus took a long trip into the countryside where the working Windmills of Kinderdijk stood. When the bus parked, the driver stood up and addressed everyone over the speakers.

A. Nation

"Ladies and gentlemen, it is over eighty-five degrees outside. I have bottled water for everyone, so please take one and if you don't have a hat, I will provide one for you. Have a nice time viewing our famous windmills. Here is your guide."

The guide took the microphone and told some of the histories of the area.

"We are in the province of South Holland, nine and a half kilometers from Rotterdam. This area you are about to visit is a UNESCO World Heritage Site established in 1997. Once we had over a hundred and fifty windmills, but now there are twenty-eight and nineteen of those are in Kinderdijk.

"They were built in 1738 from brick. The sails you see turning come within a half meter from the ground. That is why they are called, 'ground sails.' Please be careful when you walk around a functioning windmill. What you see around you as you walk along the boardwalks are wetlands. If we didn't use the windmills, I'd have to load you into boats. As you step off the bus, please turn on your receivers from the hotel to hear me talk as we go. Come, please," their guide said, reattaching the mike to the bus dash holder.

Joyce and Rosetta pulled out their expandable sunhats and secured the cords under their chins. Climbing out of the air-conditioned bus into the muggy air jolted Rosetta back into reality as she felt the small cloth purse resting under her blouse.

One at a time, the passengers disembarked off the bus, starting from the front row of seats. Some took the opportunity to take the side door to exit. Everyone gathered around their guide holding a pole with a paddle on the end. She held it out to the passengers could touch their receivers and hear their guide speak.

"Does everyone hear me, now?" she asked.

Receiving an affirmative from everyone, she marched off toward the wooden pathway. Everyone made their way down the mounded ridge pathway running between a wetland and a few reservoir ponds.

"These windmills are still in use today for draining the river into a reservoir," their guide said.

Rosetta dug out her camera, turned it on, and began taking pictures as she walked. The row of four windmills along the canal stood out the most. Ducks of unknown species quacked back at the visitors who had interrupted their solitude. The birds took flight and flew to the other bank of the channel.

"Careful, Mom," Joyce said, as she took some pictures with her cell phone. Her mother was leaning over the wooden railing.

"I am. See, I have the strap wrapped around my wrist. I'm not letting this camera get away from me," she said, displaying the camera in her hand.

The tour group approached one of the windmills prepared for their day's visit. Brick cladding surrounded the structure up to the cap on top. As soon as they entered inside through a narrow door, the tourists realized how cramped the living space around the center stairway was for the operator. Shelves lined the walls, displaying old-fashioned ceramic pottery and metal bowls. Glass covered areas protected where the Wind Turbine Technicians used to sleep and prepared their food.

Joyce climbed the narrow steps up to the second level. Rosetta followed, worrying about the safety of these old open stairways. They viewed more vintage chairs and tables around the circular flooring. With more narrow stairs heading upward, Joyce kept climbing while Rosetta stayed behind. *"Must have been short men in those days,"* she thought, looking upward where Joyce had climbed.

Rosetta had to leave. The inside of the windmill was stifling with the humidity and lack of air circulation. Making her way back down to the main floor, she stepped outside and took a breath of clean air. After a couple of minutes, Joyce walked out.

"That's so fascinating," she said. "Did you make it up to the third floor?"

"No, it's too hot in there for me."

"Let's see if they have a cool snack at the gift shop," Joyce suggested.

On the way back to their bus, they stopped and visited the local gift shop. The rest of the tour group either stopped or strolled back to their waiting buses. Rosetta and Joyce each purchased an ice cream bar. They ate their treat as fast as they could in the humid heat as they walked back to their bus.

Within a few minutes, after climbing on board, they were off again on the highway. Once in Amsterdam, their driver kept driving around several familiar city blocks. Rosetta noticed she saw some of the same buildings on the streets. The guide walked back through the aisle.

"I'm just letting you know the driver is looking for your hotel access. But we are in touch with your program director. He is helping us find your hotel," she assured.

At last, their driver came to a stop and let everyone off the bus. The passengers waited until the bus driver could unload some of their tote bags stored in the lower outside compartment of the bus. Then he said, "You'll have to walk about a block through this alleyway and turn right. We can't get the bus into this street."

As it turns out, he was right. The hotel, built in a cul de sac, prevented the bus from entering the crowded avenue. After a short walk of hauling suitcases and tote bags, the passengers entered their hotel. After they registered at the front desk, they took the elevators to locate their rooms. Bellhops kept busy hauling the larger luggage from the truck from their boat. Arriving at their room, Rosetta noticed everyone's luggage stood in the hallway in front of the passenger's hotel doors. To their dismay, their large suitcases hadn't arrived.

"Everyone's meeting for dinner. Our luggage should be here afterward," Joyce said.

"Thank goodness, we still have our carry-on totes. I guess it takes a while for the bellhops to finish delivering the suitcases. Let's go," Rosetta said.

They found Tom and his friends, Barbara and Kevin, in the hotel dining room. Joyce mentioned about the lack of their luggage.

"That's odd. I got mine. Tell you what, if your bags don't show up after dinner, just give me a ring and I'll help you locate them," he said.

"Thanks, but I'm sure they are somewhere," Rosetta said.

Conversation during dinner turned to the time their planes would leave the next morning.

"My plane takes off for South Carolina at two in the afternoon, then on home to Ohio," Tom said.

"Well, we have to be at the airport early. I think our plane takes off around eleven," Rosetta said.

"Ours does too," Kevin added.

A. Nation

Returning from dinner, Rosetta and Joyce noticed their bags still hadn't shown up. *"Would the bad guys take my bag?"* she asked herself.

"You stay here, Joyce. I'm going to have a talk with the people at the registration desk," Rosetta said and marched toward the elevators.

After explaining her problem to the desk clerk, he checked his log on their computer.

"I'm unable to locate your name in the delivered luggage. There is an unclaimed area that is scheduled to go to the other hotel in our service for the passengers from your boat."

"Good, take me there."

He signaled for a bellhop to join them and grabbed a key from under the counter.

Rosetta followed him down the hall, past the elevators. When he unlocked a storage room, they could see five suitcases sitting in the center of the floor.

"We were planning to place these bags on a truck to ship our sister hotel," the clerk said.

Rosetta spotted hers and Joyce's luggage. The clerk checked her names on the tags and released them to the bellhop.

"Take these to room 701," he said to the young man.

"I'm going with you. I'm not letting these bags out of my sight," Rosetta said and followed the bellhop back to the elevators.

Arriving at her hotel door, Rosetta saw Joyce still standing outside the door, beaming at the missing luggage. They let the porter into the room and Rosetta followed. Once he deposited their bags, Rosetta passed him a Eurodollar tip

"Would you believe the hotel was going to send our bags to another hotel?" Rosetta exclaimed.

"I'm glad you found them, Mom. I need to change out of my clothes."

After their baths, they both crawled into bed. Rosetta was too tired to do any reading and fell asleep fast

---

Their phone alarms rang at five o'clock. Joyce was first to rise while Rosetta rolled to one side and sat up on the edge of her bed. Taking turns washing up, they repacked their luggage. Stepping into the hallway, Joyce closed the room door behind them.

"We're supposed to get a snack pack since the dining room isn't open at this hour," Rosetta said as they entered the elevator.

Stopping at the registration desk to drop off their room keys, they collected a food bag from the desk clerk.

"Your transportation shall arrive in an hour. Have a nice flight," she said.

"Thank you. Let's sit over here, Joyce," Rosetta said.

Barbara and Kevin stepped out of the elevators. While Kevin finished his room arrangements, Barbara sat near Rosetta.

"Seems like we just spent a few days on the boat and now here we are," the woman said.

"Yes, our boat trip was enjoyable and memorable," Rosetta replied.

Joyce opened her sack lunch and peeked inside. "Mom, there's a sandwich, juice, an apple, and a cookie in our bags," she said.

"Better eat something now," Rosetta advised, pulling her sandwich out.

A half hour later, a white suburban showed up outside the front door of the hotel.

"Looks like our transport is here," Kevin said, rising from his chair.

Just as they stood up, they heard someone by the elevators yell, "Wait, Rosetta!"

Around the corner, Tom pulled his luggage toward them.

"I wasn't sure I'd catch you before you left," he said, taking a few deep breaths of air.

"But your plane doesn't leave until later," Rosetta said, stopping to talk.

Joyce collected their luggage and followed the others through the sliding door to give the two some time alone.

"And I didn't want you to leave before I could say goodbye. Here are my phone number and email if you want to get in touch," he said, handing her a scrap of white paper.

Rosetta accepted his information and they walked toward their transportation. The vehicle had four doors. Joyce and the others sat in the rear while Rosetta and Tom entered one of the side doors to sit in the second bench seat behind the driver. As soon as their driver finished loading their suitcases in the rear, he rounded the suburban to climb into the driver's seat.

Rosetta dug around in her carry-on tote and pulled out a small business card and a pen. She wrote something on the back.

"Here, you can contact me at the travel agency or by my cell phone," she said and offered the card to Tom.

"Everyone buckled up," their driver asked.

Receiving confirmation from everyone they had buckled their seat belts, the driver drove away from the hotel. At six o'clock in the morning, the sun hadn't risen yet. Few cars at this hour were traveling on the freeway, making the ride smooth and comfortable.

"Will Mr. Richter be able to meet us before we take off?" Rosetta asked Tom.

"He should be arriving now at the airport," Tom confirmed.

A light glow in the clouds above them signaled the dawn's early light. Tom and Kevin helped their driver hand over the luggage to their respective owners. Saying their goodbyes, Barbara and Keven walked first inside the airport terminal. Tom followed Rosetta and Joyce, rolling their bags through the sliding doorway.

Obtaining their reserved tickets at the airline counter, they dropped off their larger suitcases. Once they received their boarding passes and luggage claim stickers, they located the customs line. By now, Rosetta couldn't see the other couple who rode with them this morning. The waiting time in line didn't take too long as they were herded to the automated passport readers. From experience, after passing through the electronic machine, she paused for the security guard who stamped her passport.

As they walked down the concourse, a familiar figure approached them from behind.

"How are you two doing today?" Hans Becker asked.

"Good. I was wondering if you were going to show up," Rosetta said.

They watched for their gate numbers and after locating it, Tom set his luggage by theirs.

"Our guest should be in one of the gates up ahead. I'll look for him if you don't mind watching my bags," he said.

"No, go find him," Rosetta replied, arranging a few of their bags around their seats.

As soon as Tom took off down the terminal, Joyce asked, "Where's your reader? I want to look at his picture again."

"Yes, if you don't mind, I would like to look as well," Hans said before he took his seat.

"Oh, it's on the bottom of my carry on. No matter, I put his photo on my phone. Clever me, huh?" Rosetta said.

"What would I do without you? Let's see, I was kidnapped, chased by thieves, enamored by a handsome fraud, and had a wonderful boat ride."

"You're a funny girl. Oh, look. There's Tom with a man and a woman. Maybe she's a daughter."

Hans stood up.

The older man looked short next to Tom's lanky frame. The gray-haired woman, following the men, looked about Rosetta's age.

"Rosetta. Joyce. I want you to meet the real Aric Richter and his daughter, Kara," Tom said, gesturing for them to sit down. Hans introduced himself before shaking the elder man's hand.

Joyce moved over one seat, allowing the older man to sit between her and her mother.

"Mr. Richter, this is Rosetta. She has something to give you," Tom said.

Rosetta, still standing, pulled out the passport purse between her cleavage, removed the small black box from her carry on, and passed both objects over to the elderly gentleman.

"I hope this reunites your family and property," she said, placing the small maroon cloth into his wrinkled hands.

"Shall we sit down?" Tom asked again.

Everyone took their seats around the old man. He peeled back the layers of cloth and picked out the contents from his hand. A large red stone glittered back at him. Gasping, he held it close to his eyes.

"Kara, does this look like what I think it is?" he asked, turning toward his daughter, seated beside him.

"Let me look at it," she said and pulled out a small magnifying glass.

After a few minutes looking the jewel over, she said, "Yes, father, this is real."

She handed the bright stone back to her father who looked at it again. After he rewrapped the ruby into the satin cloth, and placed the gift into the small black box. His daughter slipped the container into her purse.

"Now, it's too late to lay claims to any lands my great grandfather once owned. With my home in Italy, I have made a wonderful life for my family and grandchildren. On the flight over here, I have decided this should be used for good."

"What will you do with it?" Joyce asked.

"My Kara, here, manages an orphanage near our home. But first, to raise more funds, I think we need to travel back to our ancestral lands and announce our find and the good we can accomplish."

"Yes, that's an excellent idea, papa. But first, let's get you home. Our plane will leave in the hour," Kara said.

When the old man stood, everyone rose and shook his hand. Tom waved them goodbye and sat back down next to Rosetta.

"I have to return to work. Thank you for giving me this opportunity to greet a heritage. I will bid you goodbye and have a safe trip home," Hans said.

A. Nation

"Thank you, you too," Rosetta replied.

Tom turned to Rosetta and filled her in about the daughter of Mr. Richter.

"His daughter told me earlier, she handles all of his affairs. Whether they will actually follow through with his plans remains to be seen.

"Well, at least we did the right thing," Rosetta said.

When the announcement about their plane came over the airport intercom, Tom said his goodbyes and watched them line up at their gate. Rosetta waved back and walked through the doorway. She turned for one more look where Tom had stood, but he had already left.

"You're going to miss him, aren't you?" Joyce said as they walked through the jetway.

"A little. Maybe we'll see each other on another trip," Rosetta replied.

Before their flight could take off, Rosetta watched through the porthole as the ground crew began removing suitcases from the cargo bay.

The pilot announced why their flight was delayed.

"Some of the passengers are not on board our airplane. Please be patient, until we have removed their luggage."

"That's right, remember Lockerbie, Scotland?" Rosetta asked, her daughter.

"Sorry, Mom," Joyce said, looking up the town and then smiled, "I wasn't born yet."

"Well, a bomb was sent on a plane by another unwilling passenger. That's why the people on the plane have to match the luggage in the cargo hold," Rosetta explained.

"That's a good idea," Joyce said and looked over toward the other seats. "Hey, isn't that the woman who took the jewels at the castle?"

"Where?" Rosetta asked, glancing around at the filled seats to her left.

"A row up."

"It's Mary, I mean Gloria. I guess they let her go. I don't see Mr. Heyburn."

Chapter 22 – Home

As soon as the ground crew finished releasing the ties, their plane began the flight back to Washington D.C. Rosetta managed to pull her reader out to begin reading another story but she couldn't sit still any longer.

"What's wrong, Mom?" Joyce asked when her mother unbuckled herself from the seat.

"I'm going to talk to Gloria."

"Don't start anything." Joyce grinned at her mother.

"I'll be good. If the snack tray comes by, get me a cookie and a drink," Rosetta said, holding the back of her chair for support.

She walked over to Gloria, who was reading the airline magazine. Rosetta sat in the empty seat beside her. She guessed that's where Mr. Heyburn would have sat.

"Gloria, may I speak to you?"

"Oh, hi, Mrs. B—I mean Mrs. Blessing. Sure."

"I'm glad the police let you go. Where's Mr. Heyburn?"

"He took the necklace. When the police showed up, they let me go. I think he's still in custody. I guess I won't have a job when I get back to D.C., will I?" Gloria said.

"You were starting to get the hang of things. Just show up and see what happens. I can't guarantee anything because we may have a new boss."

"Thanks, Mrs. Blessing, but I made more as a barmaid."

"If you put your mind to your work, you can make more and become a manager someday. Anything is possible," Rosetta said.

"Okay, I'll stay a while if the new boss takes me back. Thanks."

Rosetta smiled and rose to return to her seat.

"Everything all right?" Joyce asked.

"Yes, I guess my boss was detained. I'm just in time, here comes the snack cart."

When the overhead lights dimmed, she noticed Joyce had settled in for a long movie on the screen behind the chair back in front of them. As the hour passed, both of them drifted off to sleep over the Atlantic Ocean. She stirred in her sleep as a dream took over her thoughts.

~~~~~~~

Rosetta was glad she had the weekend to recover from the long flight. Joyce stayed the first night. After breakfast, she moved back in with her roommates.

Rosetta was unsure of returning to work but she decided to get back into the routine. As she walked through the office, many looked up and smiled at her. Sitting at her desk, she wondered who was going to run the agency since Mr. Heyburn would not be working here. One of the employees approached her desk.

"Mrs. Blessing? Uh, a Mr. Dearborn is waiting for you in Mr. Heyburn's office," she said.

"He is? Well, I'm honored. Do you know who he is?" Rosetta asked.

"No ma'am," Carol replied.

"Mr. Dearborn is the head SEO of our travel agency. I guess I'd better see what he wants."

Rosetta walked over to the director's office and knocked on the door.

"Come in," she heard a man say.

"Mr. Dearborn. I was told you want to see me?"

"Yes, please sit down," the older man replied. "Too bad about Heyburn. I had high hopes for that man."

"I was surprised myself."

"I've been looking over your work record. Very impressive. No sick days, no lateness. Do you have any plans for your future employment here?" he asked.

"Sir, before I took my vacation, I had been seriously thinking of quitting. The work had become too stressful for me."

"Hmm, and now?"

"Well, the work crew I trained seems to be running smoothly. I'll have to see how it goes."

"You could hire a new manager?"

"Then I'd have to train him and new help next year, I don't—" Rosetta was about to say.

"Her, I was thinking you could handle the job," he said.

"Me, sir?" Rosetta said, straightening in her chair.

"Yes, you did a wonderful job on training but I believe you are more suited for this office," Mr. Dearborn said, rising from the leather chair. "Try it out."

He stepped away and gestured for her to sit in the larger chair. She gripped the armrests and eased her body into the soft cushion.

"But what will I get in return?" she asked.

"Well, more pay, more vacation, a car—"

"A car? I'm sorry, sir. It's just mine is starting to wear out."

"You will have to interview for the management position, but did I mention, longer lunch hours, and meetings with heads of state."

On an impulse, Rosetta jumped out of the chair and hugged her boss.

"I'm sorry, sir. I'm just so happy."

"No, that's fine. I'll leave you to your new position. Have a nice day. Have a nice day."

~~~~~~~~

"Have a nice day," Rosetta heard the stewardess say as she walked by the cabin seats.

Their plane had just landed. Rosetta, overcome with a depressive feeling when she realized she had just been dreaming.

"Mom, you look unhappy. I thought you would love to return home," she said.

"I was, but I was dreaming of an excellent job opportunity. Now I'll have to resign and maybe find something else to do."

"Like what?" Joyce asked.

"I like discovering the truth in things. Maybe I could open my own detective agency."

"I think that's great. Maybe I could help you out."

The pilot announced over the communication system for the passengers to buckle their seatbelts. As the plane circled Dulles Airport one more time, Rosetta levered up her seat into the straight position.

After landing, Rosetta and Joyce headed to the baggage claim. They waited by the carousel of luggage moving by. Joyce grabbed her suitcase but Rosetta's bag never showed up on the carousel. Spotting an airport handler, loading luggage into a cart, she walked over to talk to him.

"What am I going to do?" Rosetta asked.

"Do you still have your baggage claim tickets?" he asked.

Joyce spoke up. "Yes, I do," she said, holding her boarding pass up with the claim stickers attached to the back.

"Good, this airline has an app you can use to track your bags or report them missing," he explained.

A. Nation

Joyce loaded the application into her cell phone and looked up the claim numbers.

"Mom, your suitcase is going to Boston," Joyce said.

"Well, that's fine and dandy. Thank you, sir, you've been a great help," Rosetta said.

The clerk nodded and pushed his loaded cart down the terminal.

"I'm sending a message to the airline. At least we know where it is," Joyce said.

"But my little souvenirs and my favorite clothes are in the suitcase," moaned Rosetta.

"I bet those men in the Amsterdam airport took your suitcase off our plane by mistake," Joyce suggested.

"But it was plainly marked for Dulles in D.C., phooey."

They walked out of the terminal to Joyce's car in the Long Term Parking lot. Rosetta called her son, Bob, to meet them at the house with Dolly.

"Did you mean it, that you would help me start my detective business?" Rosetta asked as her daughter opened the trunk of her car.

"Yes, I have one more year college to finish. I thought about teaching history at one of the local high schools, but detective work sounds more fun," Joyce said, dumping her luggage inside the trunk space.

"You should still get the school position. It would be steady work until my practice is going. Detecting would be a lot of work at first," Rosetta said, placing her carry on into the car trunk.

"I'll see what's available at that time. I know a lot of social media groups where you can get noticed," Joyce said, opening the driver's door.

"Now, I'll have to hand in my resignation at the travel agency," Rosetta sighed as she sat down.

"Mom, this will be a huge step for you. Why don't you wait and see how things go at work. You'll have a new boss and it may not be so bad," Joyce suggested, driving out of the parking lot.

"Okay, but I really want to do this. No divorce cases and no petty theft."

"Agreed. What would you call it?" Joyce asked, driving up the highway on the ramp.

"At first I thought about Blessing and Blessing but when you get married, it wouldn't work," Rosetta said.

"I know, how about A Blessing in Disguise?"

"Or Discover Your Rosetta?"

"That's funny, Mom. You'll think of something," Joyce said.

Rosetta used Joyce's phone and brought up the airline app.

"Oh, great. My suitcase is heading back to Amsterdam," she moaned.

When they arrived at Rosetta's home, her son, Bob, stepped outside the front door. He walked down the sidewalk to help them with their luggage. Rosetta gave him a hug.

"Where's your suitcase, Mom?" he asked, looking around the inside of the trunk.

"Oh, don't remind me. The airline is taking my bag on another flight back to Europe."

"I hope they return it. I've heard stories of lost luggage before," he said.

"Now, I brought your children some toys if I ever see my suitcase again."

"That's all right, Mom. They have plenty of toys," he said.

"But these are made in Germany," she stressed.

As soon as Rosetta stepped into the house, Dolly ran up to her, jumping with glee.

"You didn't have any problem with my dog, did you?" she asked her son.

"Not a bit. She got lots of love from my kids. Now I'll have to get them a dog too. They were sure unhappy when I packed Dolly up," he said.

"Bring your children over here once and a while," Rosetta suggested

"Yes, Mom. So how was your trip?" he asked.

Joyce looked at her mother.

"It was a great trip. We had a good time, didn't we, Joyce?" Rosetta asked.

"Yes, Mom, it was fantastic," Joyce said, hauling her suitcase up to her old room.

"Why do I get the feeling I'm missing the code somewhere?" he asked.

"Bob, women always talk in code. Can you stay a while and visit?"

"Sorry, Mom, I promised Kate I'd come home for dinner. See you two later," he said and left through the front door.

Rosetta closed the door behind him and removed her coat.

Joyce returned to the front room to find her brother had left. "Well, he didn't stay long. I'll stay the night, but tomorrow, I have to return to my apartment."

"Want to watch a movie?" Rosetta asked, hanging up her coat in the hall closet.

"Sure, nothing with castles, okay?"

"No castles. I'll make popcorn," Rosetta said.

On Monday morning, Rosetta walked into the travel agency. Everyone greeted her. Sitting down at her desk, she looked over the ticket schedule for the week. One of the male employees walked over to her.

"Mrs. Blessing?"

"Yes?"

"Mr. Dearborn is here. He's waiting for you in his office."

"Thank you, Boyd," she replied.

"This feels just like my dream," she thought.

Mr. Dearborn, the owner of several travel agencies in the east had aged the last time Rosetta had seen him. His graying hair had receded to expose a bald plate on top of his head and his weathered face sagged more than she remembered.

"Mr. Dearborn, you wish to see me?" Rosetta asked.

"Yes, please come and sit down by me. I don't hear so good even with these darn things in my ears. I heard you took a vacation. Sorry about Mr. Heyburn, heard his wife is suing him for divorce—First, she has to wait for the extradition."

"Yes, sir."

"Ahem, I've decided to bring a new manager in here. A man I know real well."

"A man, sir?"

"Yes, he's been with the company for over twenty years. Mr. Waters will be the new manager. And since the agency has been running so well while you were gone, I'm afraid I'll have to let you go. I have always liked your work ethic and will be happy to give you a glowing recommendation."

At first, Rosetta couldn't believe her ears. Then she started smiling. She rose out of her chair and bent over to hug Mr. Dearborn.

"Well, I–I, uh, never had that reaction from an employee whom I just fired," he said.

"I'm sorry, sir, but for a long time, I have been thinking about quitting and starting my own business. You just gave me the incentive I needed."

"Well, I'm glad—I think," he said.

A. Nation

"I'm going home now, sir, if that's all right with you. I don't think I could accomplish much here now. Is my last paycheck ready in accounting?"

"Yes, yes. And good luck to you."

Just as Rosetta opened the office door, several employees rushed away to their seats. They all had heard.

"Everyone, I want to make an announcement. As you have heard, I will be leaving this wonderful travel agency. Don't worry about me. I'll be fine. When I open my new business, you are welcome to stop by and say hello," Rosetta said and walked out of the office.

Two weeks later, while opening her mail, she noticed an envelope with the riverboat logo in the corner. Thinking she was charged for their drinks, she opened it up and drew out the letter. Reading it over twice, she gasped.

"Oh my, oh my!" she exclaimed and picked up her phone to call Joyce.

"Hi, Mom, what's up?" her daughter asked.

"You'd never guess what I just received in the mail?"

"Elephants?" teased her daughter.

"No, you have to come over when you can. You'll never believe what the riverboat company sent me."

"Okay, I'll get over there in an hour."

"Perfect," Rosetta said.

She rose from her chair and headed for her bedroom to change clothes and wash her hair. Later she returned to the kitchen where her dog, Dolly, checked her food dish. Rosetta pulled out the bag of kibble from the lower cabinet and scooped a handful into the dog dish.

Dolly started to eat but then looked up and perked her ears.

Rosetta heard the familiar tap on her back door. Joyce used her key and walked into the kitchen.

223

"Okay, Mom. What's going on?"

"Read this," Rosetta said, handing her the letter.

As Joyce started reading, her eyes grew larger. She grinned and sat down at the kitchen table.

"Well, I'll be. This is a $3400 voucher on a future trip. Are you going to use it?"

"You betcha, I will. See they felt sorry that we couldn't enjoy the full trip on the rivers due to the low water level. Come on, let's look over that brochure again," Rosetta said, setting two coffee cups on the table before taking her chair.

They looked the catalog over but couldn't decide which trip to apply the vouchers.

"I like three of them. But we have time to decide," Joyce said and picked up the newspaper lying near her coffee cup. Flipping through the pages a news story caught her eye.

"Mom, did you see this?" she asked.

"No, I haven't read the paper yet. What is it?"

"Here's a story about Mr. Richter. He was robbed!"

"What?" Rosetta said, sitting down near Joyce.

"It says here, he went on his promotion trip around Europe to raise funds for his daughter's orphanage. One night, someone broke into his hotel room and, get this, Mom, stole the ruby. Lucky for him, the money raised is safe in the bank."

"Let me see that," Rosetta said, pulling the paper closer.

"He told the policia, he had it appraised in London at One hundred thousand. Oh dear, and all that we did for that man."

"Read on, there's good news at the bottom of the story," Joyce said.

"He had raised over 195,000 Euros that is safe and sound in the bank. That is good news. That means they raised more than the ruby was worth," Rosetta said.

"I wonder who took it?" Joyce asked.

A. Nation

"Probably, another thief. Your thief should still be in jail," Rosetta replied.

"He's not my thief, Mom," Joyce said, smiling at the memory. "Come on, let's go look at that rental."

They gathered up their coffee cups and placed them in the sink. Dressing into their winter coats for the cold November day, they headed out to Joyce's car.

Alfredo, relaxing in his recliner, watched the news report. Then he threw his shoe at the TV screen, missing the screen by an inch.

"Mario!" he yelled.

His assistant peered around the doorway.

"Si, boss?"

"Find out who stole that ruby!" he yelled.

"Uh, boss, this just arrived in the post," his employee said, extending his arm to hand over an envelope.

"What's this? Well, don't just stand there, open it for me," Alfredo bellowed.

The servant reached for a letter opener from Alfredo's desk and opened the sealed letter. Handing the envelope back to his boss, Alfredo grabbed it out of his hands.

As Alfredo read the contents of the letter, his blood pressure began to rise.

"That Marco Benedetti has my ruby," he growled.

"But I heard he was put in jail," his assistant said.

Alfredo pointed at the television screen. The news people were reporting Marco's escape.

The boss uttered a few swear words in Italian.

"Now he wants me, ME, to pay him for the stone. Bring me my phone," Alfredo shouted.

The End

Thank you for reading Mystery Along the Danube. I hope you enjoyed the story as much as I enjoyed writing it. Would you please take a moment to enter a product review at: https://www.amazon.com/Mystery-Along-Italian-Coast-Barcelona/dp/B085RNLJVZ

It only takes a minute to dash off a few sentences and that helps the author improve her writing more than you realize.

.

A. Nation

Epilogue

To date, Alfredo and Interpol hadn't caught up with Marco. The story you have just read and Rosetta's historical book is fiction. The locations, occurrences with the riverboat on the rivers, the missing suitcase, and the tours are real. Stay tuned for the next Rosetta Blessing adventure as a private detective on a cruise around Italy.

About the Author

A. Nation travels the west with her husband. This is her thirteenth novel and more writing will be done.

I have always enjoyed reading science fiction and mysteries. I write about stories of the future mimicking today's social issues and/or real life events. This way I can explore issues such as greed, retribution, prejudice, political corruption, and where our future could be going. - A. Nation.

A. Nation
Contact Information

Amazon has a New Release Alert. Not only can you check out the latest deals, but also they will send you an email when A. Nation's book is released. You can follow the author here at

<u>A. Nation's book page</u>

~

Be sure to join my **VIP mailing list** to receive a notice when a new book publishes in any format or when one goes on sale through her monthly newsletter, go to <u>VIP Monthly Newsletter</u>. This will be the only time she'll contact you. No spam.

Do you follow **BookBub**? They also have a New Release Alert.

Look for my book Interview in <u>Profilecritics</u> & bargains at <u>Indie Book Lounge</u>

Take a peek at Rosetta's next exciting European trip to Italy. As she and her daughter sail around the boot, old and new nemesis disrupt her journey. Please enjoy the following escerpt I have provided for you.

Excerpt from the next Rosetta Blessing book

Margaret Trappe invited her younger sister, Anne, to spend the night together while her husband attended a meeting in another city. Her sister slept in the spare bedroom down the hall. Just as Margaret dozed off, she thought she heard her bedroom door open.

"Anne?" she called.

A shadow crossed her vision in front of her chest of drawers. The outline of a man holding a knife in the air sent her screaming as she struggled out of her bed and ran out of the bedroom. Still, in her bare feet, she pounded on Anne's bedroom door. When she looked behind her, the shadow on the wall came toward her.

"Anne let me in!" she yelled. "He's got a knife," Margaret screamed.

When she didn't receive an answer, she turned and saw the dark shadow advancing toward her. She didn't have time for her sister to answer the door. Turning toward the stairway, she ran for her life through the house out the back door into the cool spring night across the frosted grass.

Frightened, Anne rushed to the door and locked the doorknob.

"Margaret, what's happening?" she answered.

Then she heard nothing more.

Another scream rang outside of the rear of the home. Rushing to her second story window, she witnessed a woman in a long white nightgown running across the lawn. Fearful that the intruder would try to get to her, she grabbed her cell phone from the dresser near the bed and huddled in the closet. Shaking, she called the police.

The police arrived and discovered a woman's body lying face down in the frosted dirt of this past summer's garden. Anne stood crying, wrapped in a standard issue blanket from the officer's car. A policewoman guided her back to the warmth of the home and sat her down in the living room.

"Which way to your kitchen. I'll make us some coffee," she said. "Oh, and where can we locate her husband?"

"Avery? He's in Philadelphia. His hotel phone is on the desk over there," she whimpered, drying her eyes with some officer's handkerchief.

A few minutes later, Officer Riggins returned with two cups of coffee and set them down on the round commode tabletop between their chairs.

"Now, tell me exactly what happened?" the officer asked---

The leaves were turning several shades of orange and red this fall. Joyce walked into the house where her mother lived alone. She entered college for her last year studying European history but decided to move back home to help her mother open a new detective business in Alexandria.

"Mom, where are you?" she called out from the bottom of the staircase.

"In here, honey," Rosetta replied from the kitchen.

When Joyce walked into the kitchen, she noticed her mother hunched over the dining table looking at the classified ad of the newspaper.

"Looking for a new job?" Joyce asked.

"No, I'm looking for a place we can rent. I don't want strangers coming to my door."

Joyce pulled out two cups from the cupboard and picked up the warm coffee pot. Pouring the dark liquid into the cups, she searched the shelf for cookies. In a wrapper, she spotted the black and white Oreos.

Setting the coffee filled cups on the table, she returned and brought over the cookies.

"Let me help you with that, Mom," Joyce said.

"Okay, but these offices all seem expensive," Rosetta said.

"Well, we don't have to be on a main street, we're not a retail store."

"Mom, if we are working with the police and detecting and such, wouldn't we need to apply for a license of some kind?" Joyce asked.

"Yes, and I've already done that. I knew one of my neighbors had a relative in the police force, so she introduced me to him. I got the paperwork filled out and I'll receive my certificate from the county in the mail," Rosetta explained.

"Great. How about this one? It's only seven hundred dollars a month," Joyce asked.

"But look at the address. That's not the best part of town. We want to attract a better-paying clientele," Rosetta said.

"But starting out, we may need this neighborhood. Oh, here's one around five hundred plus utilities not far from here. What do you think?" Joyce asked.

Made in the USA
Columbia, SC
04 November 2020